New Sheriff in Town

"The sheriff's likely to be gone a long while, Buck," Clint said. "I can't stay here indefinitely, you know."

"Yeah, well, what about until the Graves boys come back?"

"You think you could handle this job, Buck?" Clint asked him.

"No sir."

"You don't?"

"No sir," Buck said. "I can back your play, but there ain't no way I could do the sheriff's job. Not yet, anyway. I ain't experienced enough, or good enough."

"It's a smart man who knows those things about himself, Buck."

"Thank you, sir."

And it's a smart man who knows what he has to do, Clint thought.

He took the badge out of his pocket and pinned it on.

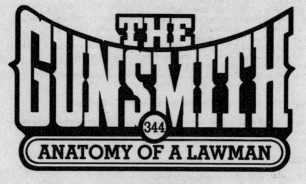

THE GUNSMITH

344

ANATOMY OF A LAWMAN

J. R. ROBERTS

JOVE BOOKS, NEW YORK

THE BERKLEY PUBLISHING GROUP
Published by the Penguin Group
Penguin Group (USA) Inc.
375 Hudson Street, New York, New York 10014, USA

Penguin Group (Canada), 90 Eglinton Avenue East, Suite 700, Toronto, Ontario M4P 2Y3, Canada
(a division of Pearson Penguin Canada Inc.)
Penguin Books Ltd., 80 Strand, London WC2R 0RL, England
Penguin Group Ireland, 25 St. Stephen's Green, Dublin 2, Ireland (a division of Penguin Books Ltd.)
Penguin Group (Australia), 250 Camberwell Road, Camberwell, Victoria 3124, Australia
(a division of Pearson Australia Group Pty. Ltd.)
Penguin Books India Pvt. Ltd., 11 Community Centre, Panchsheel Park, New Delhi—110 017, India
Penguin Group (NZ), 67 Apollo Drive, Rosedale, North Shore 0632, New Zealand
(a division of Pearson New Zealand Ltd.)
Penguin Books (South Africa) (Pty.) Ltd., 24 Sturdee Avenue, Rosebank, Johannesburg 2196,
South Africa

Penguin Books Ltd., Registered Offices: 80 Strand, London WC2R 0RL, England

This is a work of fiction. Names, characters, places, and incidents either are the product of the author's imagination or are used fictitiously, and any resemblance to actual persons, living or dead, business establishments, events, or locales is entirely coincidental.

ANATOMY OF A LAWMAN

A Jove Book / published by arrangement with the author

PRINTING HISTORY
Jove edition / August 2010

Copyright © 2010 by Robert J. Randisi.
Cover illustration by Sergio Giovine.

ISBN: 978-0-515-14828-2

JOVE®
Jove Books are published by The Berkley Publishing Group,
a division of Penguin Group (USA) Inc.,
375 Hudson Street, New York, New York 10014.
JOVE® is a registered trademark of Penguin Group (USA) Inc.
The "J" design is a trademark of Penguin Group (USA) Inc.

PRINTED IN THE UNITED STATES OF AMERICA

10 9 8 7 6 5 4 3 2 1

ONE

Sheriff Jack Harper gritted his teeth at the pain. He was lying on his belly on a table in Doc Foster's surgery while the doctor was digging into his back for two bullets the Graves gang had put there earlier in the day.

"Damn it, Doc!" Harper said.

"Lie still, ya damned fool!" Doc Foster growled.

"Are your hands shakin', you old drunk?" Harper demanded.

"Shut up," Doc said from between his own clenched teeth.

"Buck, you there?" Harper asked his deputy.

"I'm here, Sheriff."

"Is that old man drunk?" Harper demanded. "Is he tryin' to dig bullets out of my back while he's drunk? Shoot him if he is. Shoot him before he kills me. Argh!!!"

"He ain't drunk, Sheriff," Buck Wilby said. "Honest, he ain't."

The truth was Doc Foster didn't have any whiskey at all in him. It was the only way he could have dug the slugs out of Harper's back without his hands shaking.

But even with steady hands, he could not get to the bullets. The two slugs of lead had both ended up perilously close to the sheriff's spine. If Foster dug any more, he'd paralyze the man for life.

Despite the fact they were sniping at each other, the forty-five-year-old lawman and sixty-six-year-old doctor had been good friends for over twelve years.

"Damn it!" Foster finally snapped.

"Take it easy, Doc," the sheriff said. "You ain't really hurtin' me that much."

That was the point when the sheriff passed out.

"Doc, is he—" Buck asked.

"He's alive, but that might not make him happy," Foster said. "I've got to sew him up."

"But . . . you ain't got any lead out."

"And I can't get it out," Foster said. "If I keep tryin', he won't ever walk again. He needs surgery in a hospital."

"Where?" Buck asked. "What hospital?"

"Preferably somethin' in a big city," Foster said.

"You gonna tell 'im, Doc?" Buck asked.

"Of course I'm going to tell him, you idiot," Foster said. "Get out of here. Go over to the hotel and get him a room with a good bed."

"Yessir."

Foster knew that his friend spent most nights on a cot inside his own jail, but he was going to need a good mattress to lie on.

Damn it, Jack, he thought, I'm sorry I'm not a better doctor, my friend.

Harper came back to consciousness slowly, and when he was finally about to focus his eyes, he realized he was lying in his stomach.

"Doc?"

"I'm here, Jack."

"Well, get over here where I can see your ugly face," Harper yelled. "What the hell happened?"

Doc Foster moved to where his friend could see him.

"I'm sorry, Jack," he said. "I couldn't do it."

"What?"

"I'm not good enough to get those bullets out," Foster said. "You need a surgeon in a good hospital for that."

"Hospital?" Harper said. "I ain't got any money for a hospital, Doc."

"Don't worry about it," Foster said. "The town's gonna pay for the surgery."

"The town?" Harper asked. "Jesus, how'd you work that out?"

"I threatened 'em, and blackmailed 'em."

"Threatened?"

"I told the Council if they didn't pay for the surgery, they were going to lose a lawman, and a doctor. I also told them they'd be sitting ducks when the Graves gang came back."

"And who'd you blackmail?"

"You don't wanna know."

"Well, thanks, Doc . . . I guess."

"Don't thank me, Jack," Foster said. "If I was a better doctor—"

"Don't beat yourself up, Doc," Harper said. "You're a country doctor. That's all you ever claimed to be, and you're a good one."

"Well . . . I can arrange to get you to a hospital in Kansas City, or Saint Louis, as soon as—"

"No, not yet, Doc," Harper said.

"Whataya mean, not yet?" Foster asked. "We need to get that lead out of you as soon as possible. If they move, you can be paralyzed for life, or they could kill you."

"Not yet, Doc," Harper said. "You were right about one more thing."

"What's that?"

"This town is a sitting duck for the Graves gang with me gone."

"You have a deputy—"

"Buck would be dead in the first ten seconds," Harper said.

"Then the town will have to hire a replacement."

"I don't think so."

"What are you proposing, then?"

"I'm gonna pick my own replacement," Harper said, "and I'm not leavin' town until he gets here."

"What kind of fool—"

"Take down this telegram, Doc, and I'll tell you where to send it."

"You already got your replacement picked out?"

"Oh yeah," Jack Harper said. "I just hope he'll do it."

TWO

When Clint rode into Guardian, Missouri, he thought he had stepped back in time. The town looked like Dodge or Tombstone in their prime. The streets were teeming with people and wagons, corrals were filled with cattle or horses. Outside of town he had seen another herd, which he found odd. Because he had recently taken part in what was supposed to have been the last great trail drive.

The telegram that had summoned him here had come from an old friend, a lawman named Jack Harper. He knew that Harper had been the law in Guardian for about a dozen years, but he had never managed to visit him here, and had never before received a telegram. The last time he had seen Harper had been about fourteen years ago, when they had ridden in a posse together in Colorado.

Guardian's busy main street was pitted with holes and trenches, further indication of how well traveled it was. Not that he needed further proof. The fact that he had to steer Eclipse in and around different kinds of traffic was indication enough.

He found the sheriff's office and reined Eclipse in. He dismounted, tied the horse off, and stepped up onto the boardwalk. When he walked into the office, it was another odd moment, as if he'd stepped into a sheriff's office twenty years earlier. Many towns had updated their jails, and some had even modernized their law to include police stations, with uniformed men and a police chief. But he didn't see any sort of modernization here.

There was a small rolltop desk up against one wall, a gun rack on the wall next to it. The office was empty, in need of a sweep, especially back in the cell block, which had three cells, all empty.

When the office door opened, he turned and saw a young man enter. He had a deputy sheriff's badge pinned to his shirt.

"Can I help ya?" the man asked.

"I'm looking for Sheriff Harper."

The man immediately looked suspicious.

"Why?"

"He's an old friend," Clint said, "and he sent for me." He held up the telegram.

Now the deputy looked surprised.

"You came?"

"I guess so," Clint said. "I'm here."

"You're Clint Adams?"

"That's right."

"Wow," Buck said. "The sheriff said you'd come. I'm Buck Wilby, the deputy."

"He was right. You the only deputy?"

"Only one he has right now."

"Where is Jack?"

"The sheriff is across the street at the Westgate Hotel," Buck said.

"Should I just wait for him here, then?"

"Uh, no, I think he'd want you to go across the street and see him."

"Okay," Clint said, "tell him I'll come and see him after I see to my horse and get myself a room."

"The livery is right down the street," Buck said, "but you

already have a room waiting for you across the street—no charge."

"Is that a fact?" Clint wondered what he had done already to rate a free room.

Buck and Clint stepped outside the sheriff's office.

"I'll walk my horse up to the livery and be right back."

"The sheriff's gonna be real glad to see you, Mr. Adams."

They walked their separate ways.

THREE

When Clint walked into the hotel lobby carrying his saddlebags and rifle, there were several people checking in at the desk. However, Buck Wilby was coming across the lobby toward him.

"I got your room key for ya, Mr. Adams," the deputy said.

"Just call me Clint, Buck," Clint said.

"Okay, Clint. You're in room five."

"And where's Jack?"

"He's in room eleven."

"He's living in the hotel?"

"Um, not exactly livin'," Buck said. "You'll see when you go up. Ya want me to take your gear to your room?"

Clint took his key from the deputy and said, "I'll take my stuff to my room myself. Then I'll go to Jack's room."

"Well, okay," Buck said. "Just knock on the door when you're ready."

"I can do that," Clint said, and headed up the stairs, aware that the people checking in were frowning at him. How did he get a room ahead of them, they were probably wondering. One of them was a pretty young woman who was watching Clint for a different reason.

* * *

Clint checked his room, found it satisfactory. His window overlooked the main street, and there was no access from there.

He tossed his saddlebags onto the bed, and leaned his rifle in a corner. He wondered what all the secrecy was about, but figured he might as well go to room eleven and find out.

He left his room, walked down the hall, and knocked. The door was opened by an older man with white chin whiskers and watery blue eyes.

"Yes?"

"Sorry," Clint said, "I must have the wrong room. I was told I'd find the sheriff in this room."

"Sheriff Harper is here," the man said. "Who wants him?"

"My name is Clint Adams," Clint said. "Jack sent for me."

"So he did."

"Let him in, you old reprobate!" Jack Harper shouted from inside the room.

"You heard him," the man said. "Come on in. I'm Doctor Foster."

"Doctor?" Clint asked, stepping into the room.

Clint saw a man lying prone on a bed, facedown, and the room had the smell of illness, or injury.

"Jack?"

"That you, Clint?" Harper asked. "Come around here where I can see you."

Clint looked at the doctor, who nodded. He walked around to the side of the bed, where he and Sheriff Harper could see eye to eye.

"Clint, good to see you. Sorry I can't get up," Harper said.

"What happened, Jack?"

"A couple of the Graves boys came in to shoot up the town, maybe rob the bank," Harper said. "I stopped 'em, but they shot me in the back."

"Twice," the doctor said.

Clint turned to the doctor.

"You get the lead out?"

"I can't," Doctor Foster said. He held his hands out. "I'm not good enough. If I go diggin' in his back, I'll paralyze him. He needs a surgeon and a real hospital."

"Then why don't you get him to one?" Clint demanded.

"He wouldn't go until you got here and he could talk to you."

Clint looked at Harper.

"Jack?"

"He's right," Harper said. "Don't blame the old goat. He tried to get me to go."

"What's so important that you had to talk to me before you get two bullets out of your back?" Clint asked.

"Hey Doc?" Harper called.

"Yeah?"

"Why don't you take a walk and let me talk to my friend?"

"I'll be out in the hall," Foster said, not offended at all. "Call if you need me."

"Okay, Doc."

Foster went out into the hall and pulled the door shut.

"My best friend in town," Jack Harper said. "It's killin' him that he can't help me."

"Apparently he's managed to keep you alive."

"At least he's done that," Harper said, "but my back hurts like hell."

"So what do you want from me, Jack?"

"I need your help, Clint," Harper said. "I need somebody to wear my badge until I come back."

FOUR

"So you want me to help you find a replacement?" Clint asked.

"No," Harper said. "You know what I'm talking about, Clint. I want you to replace me until I get back."

"Jack—"

"You haven't been in town that long, have you?" Harper asked.

"No, I just got to town about half an hour ago," Clint said. "I spoke to your deputy, but he didn't have much to tell me."

"That's because I told him not to say anythin'," Harper said. "I wanted to tell you myself."

"Look, Jack," Clint said, "I can help you, but I can't—"

"This town is a throwback, Clint," Harper said. "It needs a firm hand."

"There are plenty of other men out there with a firm hand."

"Yeah, but you're here now," Harper said.

"That's because I didn't know what I was walking into."

"Exactly."

"You sent me a telegram that asked me to come, but didn't say why," Clint said. "You tricked me."

"I need you, Clint!" Harper said. "If you turn me down, I'll have to keep lookin', and I won't have time to get these slugs out of my back."

"You're crazy, Jack," Clint said. "Leave your deputy in charge and go to the hospital—where? In Kansas City? Somewhere else?"

"Doc says Kansas City, but Buck can't handle the job. It's too big for him."

"It's just a town—"

"I told you," Harper said. "This is no normal town. This is how Abilene used to be. Tombstone. Dodge. You get it?"

"I know what you're saying, but—"

"And the Graves boys ain't done!" Harper said, cutting him off again.

"What?"

"They're coming back, and with more men," Harper said. "More family."

"Did you kill any of them?"

"I don't know," Harper said. "I know I hit at least one, but I was shootin' from my belly."

"And how many are coming back?"

"I don't know."

"And when?"

"I don't know that either," Harper said, "but somebody needs to get this town ready for them. Buck can't do that, and I don't have the time to look for someone else."

"Don't you have somebody in town—a leader—who could take your place?"

"No," Harper said. "Doc's on the Town Council and he's talked to them, but none of them can handle a gun, and they don't know what to do to get ready for the gang to come back."

"Jack," Clint said, "this is unfair. If I say no, you could end up dead before you find someone else."

"I know that," Harper said. "I tricked you into comin'. I

admit it. But that's how desperate I am to keep this town safe. I've been the law here for twelve years, Clint. If word gets out that I'm gone, who knows what will happen?"

"You mean, besides the Graves gang?"

"Yeah," Harper said. "Trouble could come from anybody."

Clint stared down at his friend. Harper was sweating and looked pale. The bandages on his back showed some blood leakage.

"Damn you, Jack—"

"My badge is on that table, Clint, right there next to you."

Clint looked down, saw the star sitting on the table next to the bed.

"Come on, Clint," Harper said. "Pick it up."

Clint picked it up.

"Pin it on."

Clint hefted the tin in his hand, then put it in his shirt pocket.

"I'll hang on to it until I can think of something," Clint said.

"I guess I'll accept that."

"You have to let the doctor take you to Kansas City," Clint said.

"I will," Harper said, "as long as you tell me you'll either pin the badge on, or find somebody to pin it on who can do the job."

"I promise, Jack."

Harper heaved a sigh of relief, then said, "Good. Now maybe you should tell the doc to get in here. I need somethin' for this pain."

Instead of calling the doctor in, Clint stepped out into the hall.

"He wants something for the pain," he said.

"Finally," Doc Foster said. "He wouldn't let me give him anythin' because he wanted to be alert when you got here."

"Before you go in, Doc," Clint said, "what are his chances?"

"Here, he has no chance," Foster said. "In a good hospital, with a good surgeon, I give him fifty-fifty."

"That'll he'll die?"

"Fifty-fifty that he'll walk," Foster said, "if he doesn't die."

"I see."

Clint took the badge out of his pocket and looked at it.

"You gonna pin it on?" Foster asked.

"I'm thinking about it."

"Take the advice of an old man," Foster said, putting his hand on the doorknob.

"What's that?"

"Don't think about it for too long."

Doc Foster went into the room.

FIVE

Clint left the hotel and went to the nearest saloon. It was midafternoon, and the Dust Cutter Saloon was doing a bang-up business. Tables were full, the bar was busy, and girls were working the floor.

"Whataya have?" the bartender asked.

"Beer," Clint said, "nice and cold."

"Onliest kind we got, mister," the bartender assured him.

The barkeep brought him his beer and went about his job, which suited Clint. He didn't need a nosy bartender chattering at him right now.

He was mad.

He was angry at Jack Harper for getting himself shot in the back, and he was angry at his friend for tricking him, inviting him to Guardian under false pretenses.

The sheriff's badge felt heavy in his shirt pocket. He'd worn a badge early in his life, but quickly learned what a thankless job it was to be a town or county sheriff. You were expected to do your job to the best of your ability, which was no problem. It was when you needed a little extra help—some extra deputies or a posse—that you learned you were on your own.

He expected nothing different from the town of Guardian. If Jack Harper expected this town to stand up for itself against a gang of gunmen, he was in for a disappointment. Then again, he'd been sheriff here for twelve years. He knew the town better than Clint did. Maybe that wasn't the case here. Maybe things were different.

Yeah, right.

Clint decided to listen to some of the talk going on around him. Eventually, among all the inane conversation that went on in a saloon, he picked out a conversation about the Graves gang.

". . . ain't the sheriff's fault they's gonna be comin' back here," one man said.

"It ain't? He shot one of 'em, didn't he?" a second man asked.

"Sure he did," a third man said, "but they was robbin' the bank."

"And didn't they put two slugs in his back?" the first man asked.

"Which is gonna make him useless when the gang comes back," the second man said. "We're gonna be sittin' ducks for them Graves boys, and it's his fault. Too bad he didn't die from them slugs."

Clint almost went looking for the men. They must have been standing at the bar somewhere. He held himself back, though. They were only proving what he'd already thought. At least one man would rather have had the sheriff dead, thinking that would save them from a gang. Clint had dealt with gangs like this all his life. They'd ride into town, kill the lawmen, and then either take over the town or burn it.

He was thinking of packing up and leaving town right then and there. Let the town fend for itself, but this town meant a lot to Jack Harper. He couldn't just walk away and leave it to be destroyed.

"The sheriff'll take care of us," the first man said. "He always does, ya know."

"That's right," the third man said. "He ain't never let us down before, has he?"

"I'm havin' another beer," the second man said. "I wanna be dead drunk when them Graves boys ride in here and burn us down."

"No tellin' when they'll come back," the first man said.

"Well, I'm gonna be drunk 'til then," the second man said. "And you mark my words. I ain't the only one in town blames the sheriff for this. There's members of the Town Council feel the same."

Again, Clint almost went looking for the three men, to find out from the one with the big mouth just who on the Council felt that way, but he decided against it. Doc Foster was on the Council. He'd just ask him.

Deputy Buck Wilby came in at that point, looked around, and spotted Clint at the bar. When Clint saw him approaching, he quickly ordered the young man a cold beer.

"Here you go, Deputy," Clint said, handing it to him.

"Are you gonna do it, Mr. Adams?"

"Do what?"

"You know," Buck said, "take the sheriff's place while he's gone."

"The sheriff's likely to be gone a long while, Buck," Clint said. "I can't stay here indefinitely, you know."

"Yeah, well, what about until the Graves boys come back?"

"You think you could handle this job, Buck?" Clint asked him.

"Nossir."

"You don't?"

"Nossir," Buck said. "I can back your play, but there ain't no way I could do the sheriff's job. Not yet anyway. I ain't experienced enough, or good enough."

"It's a smart man who knows those things about himself, Buck."

"Thank you, sir."

And it's a smart man who knows what he has to do, Clint thought. He took the badge out of his pocket and pinned it on.

SIX

While they drank their beers, the three men somewhere along the bar continued their discussion, and suddenly the big mouth had some support.

"Glen's right," a fourth voice pitched in.

"Yeah," a fifth man said, "why didn't the sheriff just let 'em go?"

"And let 'em rob the bank?" the first man asked. "Don't you got money in the bank, Hank?"

"Sure, I do," Hank said, "and I wanna be alive to get it out."

"And I want it to be standin' when I'm ready to get it," Glen said. "But that ain't gonna happen when the Graves gang gets here."

"Goddamned idiots!" Buck said, and before Clint could stop him, the young deputy went looking for the men.

"Glen Parks, you're a blamed fool!" he snapped, moving down the bar. "If it wasn't for the sheriff, this town probably woulda been burned to the ground a long time ago, so you shut yer damned mouth!"

"Oh, here's the loyal deputy, boys," Parks said. "And where was you when the sheriff got two in the back, Buck?" the man asked.

"Hidin' somewhere, I bet," Hank said, and the men laughed, even the ones who had been defending Sheriff Harper.

"Goddamnit, Parks!"

"Go ahead, boy," Parks said, "skin that iron. Who you got to back your play now that the sheriff's flat on his back?"

"Will I do?" Clint asked, stepping forward.

Suddenly the saloon got very quiet.

The five men looked at Clint as he stepped forward. The sheriff's star on his chest loomed large.

"This here's the temporary sheriff," Buck said. "He's gonna be around until Sheriff Harper gets back on his feet."

"Is that a fact?" Glen Parks asked.

Clint could have picked Parks out of the five. The man with the big mouth had a sullen face and mean eyes. About forty-five, Clint was sure this man had caught as many beatings as he'd meted out in his life.

"And do you two think yer gonna be able to defend this town against the Graves boys and their gang?"

"Sure we are," Clint said. "Because you're going to help."

"What?"

Clint noticed they were the center of attention now, and took advantage of it.

"And so are you," he said, pointing to another man, "and you, and you, and you. All of you are going to help. Otherwise you're right, this town will be burned to the ground."

"Whataya mean?" Parks demanded. "That ain't our job. It's yours!"

"Since when is it not a man's job to defend his home?" Clint asked.

"Since we pay Jack Harper—and now you—forty a month," Parks said.

"Forty a month?"" Clint asked. "That's twenty for each slug he's got in his back. And he wouldn't leave town to get those bullets taken out in a hospital until he got somebody to take his place. He wanted to make sure this town had a fighting chance when the Graves gang returned."

"And we're gonna have that with you?" Parks asked.

"We sure are," Buck Wilby said. "Let me introduce you to the new sheriff, boys. Meet Clint Adams."

SEVEN

The entire saloon seemed to be staring at Clint.

"The Gunsmith?" Parks asked.

"That's right."

"You're our new sheriff?" someone asked.

"Temporary sheriff," Buck said. "Just 'til Sheriff Harper gets back on his feet."

Someone pushed through the crowd to face Buck and Clint. He was wearing a suit, was well spoken, and Clint assumed he was one of the town fathers.

"You can't just appoint yourself sheriff of this town."

This was the first time Clint realized that Jack Harper was the town sheriff, not the county sheriff.

"I'm assuming this will go before your Town Council," Clint said, "but for now, Sheriff Harper has asked me to take over."

"Well, whatta we got to worry about, then!" somebody shouted. "The Gunsmith'll take care of them Graves boys."

"Like I was telling these gents here," Clint said, indicating Parks and his friends, "I'm here to help. I'm not here to face this gang alone. I'm not a gun for hire."

"You ain't?" somebody asked.

"If I was," Clint said, "it would cost you a hell of a lot more than forty a month."

"Now look," said the man in the suit, "before we talk about whether this man will or will not do, we have to have a meeting of the Council to see if we approve his wearing the badge."

There was some murmuring, and some laughter, and someone shouted, "Why would you not approve of the Gunsmith wearing that badge?"

"Because he wasn't duly elected to do so!" the man said. He turned to Clint. "Adams, I'm going to convene a meeting of the Council. I assume you'll be there?"

"Just tell me when and where," Clint said. "I'll either be at the sheriff's office or in the hotel across the street."

"Fine," the man said, and walked on.

The man left, and before the rest of the men in the saloon could surround Clint and bombard him with questions, he grabbed Buck's arm and pulled him out of the saloon as well.

"Who was that man?"

"Parks? He's nobody—"

"No, the man in the suit," Clint said. "Obviously he's a member of the Town Council."

"Oh yeah, that's Mr. Radke," Buck said. "He owns a bunch of businesses around town. In the last election he ran for mayor and lost, but yeah, he's on the Council."

"Is he going to be trouble?" Clint asked.

"He just always has to have a say in what's goin' on," Buck said. "He'll make a lot of noise, but in the end he'll go along with the Council."

"And how's the Council going to react to Sheriff Harper passing his badge to me?"

"Well, Doc's on the Council and his word carries a lot of weight."

"More weight that Radke's?"

"Oh yeah," Buck said, "a lot more weight than Mr. Radke's."

Clint shook his head.

"I better go over to the hotel and let Jack know what's happening already."

"He'll just be happy to see you wearin' that badge . . . Sheriff."

"Yeah, well, let's see just how long I'll be holding on to it."

Clint knocked on the door of room eleven again. It was opened by Doc Foster, who looked at him with raised eyebrows.

"Trouble already?"

"Is he awake?"

"No," Foster said. "I gave him somethin' for the pain and he's out."

"The Town Council is apparently convening to decide if I should wear this badge or not."

"And whose bright idea was that?"

"A man named Radke."

The doctor waved his hand.

"Don't worry about him," he said. "I can overrule him."

"What about the rest of the Council?"

"When they hear who you are, nobody will object—as long as you're takin' the same forty a month, that is."

"I'm doing this as a favor to Jack," Clint pointed out.

"You got the forty a month comin'," the Doc said. "And you'll earn it."

"So you'll be at the meeting?"

"Don't worry," Foster said. "I'll see you there."

EIGHT

Clint went to the sheriff's office to await word of the Town Council meeting. While he was there, he looked through Jack Harper's desk, found some wanted posters. He was leafing though them when Buck Wilby came walking in.

"I just did my rounds, Sheriff," Buck said. "What should I do next?"

"First, don't call me Sheriff," Clint said. "Just call me Clint."

"Okay, Clint. What do you want me to do next?"

"What does the sheriff usually have you do?"

"Um, just drift around town and keep an eye out for trouble."

And how often do you find trouble?"

"Uh, not that much really," Buck said, "except on weekends, when the cowpokes and drifters come into town and get liquored up."

"Okay, well, why don't you just do what you usually do?" Clint said. "Meanwhile, give some thought to who in this town would be useful when the Graves gang comes back."

"Me?" Buck asked. "You want me to recommend somebody?"

"You know the people in this town," Clint said. "I don't. Come up with some names and we'll talk about them. Okay?"

"Okay, Sher—I mean, Clint."

Buck went out the door and pulled it closed behind him. Clint looked down at the pile of wanted posters on the desk, then opened a drawer and put them away. He decided to check the weapons in the rifle rack, found them in need of cleaning. He was just about to begin when Doc Foster came in.

"Hey, Doc," he said. "How's Jack?"

"I'm takin' him on the first stage tomorrow," Doc said. "Then to the train. I'll need some help carryin' him from his room. I need four men, because we have to hold him steady."

"You got me," Clint said, "provided I'm still here."

"About that," Doc said. "You should walk over to the Council meeting with me . . . now."

"Fine," Clint said, replacing the rifle in the rack. "Let's get this over with."

Doc Foster walked Clint over to the two-story brick City Hall. They walked in and Doc led him to a room in the back.

There was a long table with five chairs, four of which were occupied. Doc Foster walked around the table and sat in the fifth chair.

"Have a seat, Mr. Adams," said a man whom Clint didn't recognize.

He only knew Doc Foster and the man from the saloon, Radke.

There was an empty chair in front of the table and Clint sat down in it.

The man seated at the other end of the table introduced himself. "I'm Hal Finley, mayor of Guardian." He was in his sixties, well dressed and healthy looking.

"Mr. Mayor," Clint said, nodding.

"You know the two men to my left, Doctor Foster and George Radke," the mayor said. "To my right are Mr. Lew Preston and Mrs. Henry Dennison."

Preston was a sad-looking man in his forties. Mrs. Dennison was a handsome-looking woman of about forty.

"Mrs. Dennison is here representing her husband, who died last year."

Clint wondered why the mayor thought that was important enough to mention.

"Mr. Adams, we understand Sheriff Harper has asked you to take his place until he's back on his feet."

"That's not quite right, Mr. Mayor."

"Oh?"

"He may never get back on his feet," Clint said. "I told him I'd wear this badge until I found someone who could handle the job."

"Well, you understand that the Town Council has to approve you as temporary sheriff."

"I understand that's a formality," Clint said.

"Actually, it's quite serious—"

"Mr. Mayor," Clint asked, "do you intend to go out into the street with a gun when the Graves gang comes back?"

"Well . . . I don't use a gun, Mr.—"

"What about you, ma'am?" Clint asked.

"Certainly not, Mr. Adams," she said. "You definitely have my vote to keep that badge."

"We haven't put this up for a vote yet—" Radke started.

"None of you plan to take up a gun when the gang gets here," Clint said, "so there's no way you're going to take this badge away from me—and there's no way I'm going to jump through your hoops." He stood up. "I intend to do what I told Jack Harper I'd do."

He turned and walked to the door, pausing for a moment.

"But I may just be calling on some of you to pick up a gun, whether you want to or not."

He left them all there staring as he went out the door.

NINE

Clint was sitting at Sheriff Jack Harper's desk when the door to the office opened and the deputy came walking in.

"Buck."

"How'd it go?" Buck asked.

Clint looked down at his chest.

"I've still got the badge on," he said, "but I don't know for how long."

"What did you tell them?"

"Basically," Clint said, "to mind their own business and stay off my back."

"Really?" Buck grinned. "I really would have liked to see that."

Clint grinned back at him.

"They weren't very happy. What's going on around town?"

"Not much," Buck said. "Folks are talking; about the sheriff gettin' shot and the Graves gang comin' back. They're wonderin' who's gonna stop them."

"Let them wonder," Clint said. "Meantime, you got any names for me?"

Buck looked down at his feet.

"Not yet," he said. "I'm still thinkin' on it."

"That's okay," Clint said. "Just let me know when you come up with somebody."

"Yes, sir," Buck said. "I'll just . . . keep makin' rounds."

"You do that, Buck."

Buck nodded and left the office.

It was a half an hour later when the door opened again and Doc Foster came in.

"They send you to collect the badge?" Clint asked.

"You didn't make yourself any friends in that room," Foster said, "but no. They voted to let you keep it."

"I wonder who they would have sent to take it if they'd voted the other way?"

"That's just it," Foster said. "Nobody was willing to try."

Clint laughed.

"I'm gonna be leavin' tomorrow with Jack, Clint," Foster said. "You're gonna have to find yourself some allies in this town."

"I've got Buck," Clint said.

"He's young."

"He'll do," Clint said. "And he's gonna help me find some others. Come to think of it, Doc. You got any suggestions before you go, I'd like to hear them."

"Suggestions?"

"For men who'll fight," Clint said. "Or for men willing to fight."

"I'll give it some thought and let you know in the mornin'," Foster said.

"Good," Clint said. "I'd appreciate it."

"I'll stop in here first thing."

"Can I come by and see Jack?"

"Let him rest," Doc said. "Why don't you wait until mornin', when you come to help move him?"

"Okay," Clint said. "What time?"

"Whenever the stage comes in," Foster said. "It'll be stoppin' right in front of the hotel."

"See you tomorrow, then."

Doc Foster nodded and left the office. Clint leaned back in his chair and put his feet up on the desk. There wasn't much else to do at this point.

Twenty minutes after Doc Foster left, the door opened a third time. Mrs. Henry Dennison entered, looked around, and paused when her eyes fell on Clint, who was standing at the stove, waiting for a pot of coffee to be ready.

"Mrs. Dennison," Clint said. "Don't tell me you've come to take the badge away from me?"

"Hardly," she said, closing the door behind her. "I just thought I'd come by for a little . . . talk. And my name is Lucy."

Clint stood up. Lucy Dennison had returned home first, put on a new dress, and fixed her hair and makeup. He had originally thought her a handsome woman of about forty. Now she was an attractive woman in her late thirties.

"Besides, they'd never trust me with anything so important," she said. "I'm just filling my husband's chair until his term of service is over."

"Then what brings you here?" Clint asked.

"Like I said," she answered, "I just wanted to . . . talk."

Twice she had hesitated before saying the word "talk." Clint had the feeling the woman had more than that on her mind.

TEN

"Can I get you a cup of coffee?"

"I suppose that'll do for a start," she said. "May I sit?"

"Take the chair at the desk," he said. "It's more comfortable."

She sat down, draping the shawl she'd been wearing over the back of the chair. Her dress was simple, blue, but it just barely covered her shoulders, and showed a shadowy valley between her breasts. It fit tightly, showing her to have a body that had probably once been trim but, as she got older, was filling out nicely.

He poured two cups of coffee, handed her one, and then perched a hip on the desk so that he was looming over her.

She tasted the coffee and said, "It's very strong. I like it."

"I'm afraid I'm used to making coffee on the trail," he said.

"No, no, it's fine," she said, putting the mug down on the desk.

"What did you want to talk to me about?"

"Well," she said, "if you're going to be our sheriff for a while, I just thought we should get acquainted. I rather enjoyed the way you handled the members of the Council earlier today. You're quite right that none of them intends to lift a finger to try to defend this town. They expect you to do that."

"That's usually what people expect when they hire a sheriff," he said, "but sometimes it's not that easy. A sheriff and his deputies can't always do these things themselves. Sometimes they need help from the town."

"Oh, I'm sure you'll find men willing to fight," she said. "Just not from the Council. They're businessmen and politicians."

"I understand that," Clint said. "What was your husband like?"

"Oh, he was like them," she said. "We owned the General Store, and Henry sat on the Town Council for years. I'm afraid most of the everyday work was left to me while he attended meetings, which usually took place in the back room of a saloon, or in a whorehouse."

"I see," Clint said. "Why would he be spending time at a whorehouse when he had a woman like you at home?"

She blushed a bit, a nice rosy hue tingeing the exposed skin of her shoulders and chest.

"My husband's appetites were something of a surprise to me," she said. "Let's just say he needed to find his pleasures somewhere else."

"I'm sorry to hear that," Clint said. "How did he die?"

"He had a heart attack while he was with a whore," she said. "Fitting, I think. But tell me about you. What brought you here?"

"Sheriff Harper sent for me, asked me to wear his badge while he was away, as a favor."

"Sounds like you're a good friend to have," she said.

"I try to be."

"Well, I suppose this town will benefit from the friendship between you and Jack Harper."

"I hope that's the way it turns out."

She stood up without drinking any more of her coffee.

"Well, I suppose I should let you get back to your work."

"I'm just sort of getting to know the office a bit," he admitted.

"I hope we can get to know each other a little better, too, while you're here."

"I'd like that, Mrs. Dennison."

"No, no," she said, "you have to call me Lucy."

"All right, Lucy,"

She started for the door, then stopped and turned back.

"Perhaps we can have dinner together one night?" she asked. "After you get yourself settled in."

"That sounds like a good idea."

"Wonderful," she said. "We'll talk about it another time."

"I'll look forward to it."

She smiled, nodded, and left the office.

Clint poured himself some more coffee and sat down at the desk. He hoped that the visits were done and that no one else from the Town Council would show up. Buck would be back soon, and he hoped the young man would have some suggestions of men who could use a gun and would be willing to stand against the Graves gang.

Clint finished his coffee, then decided to take a turn around town himself. He'd kept his gun strapped on the whole time he was in the office, so he grabbed his hat and headed out the door.

He heard the shot, and then a bullet slapped into the wooden door.

ELEVEN

Clint hit the ground, rolled, and came to a stop in front of a horse trough. There was another shot and water splashed when the bullet hit.

He heard somebody running toward him, and when he looked, he saw it was Buck.

"Buck! Get down!" Clint shouted.

Buck stopped short, unsure about what to do. Other people on the street had scattered, taking cover wherever they could. Buck was still confused when a bullet struck the ground in front of him. That unfroze him and he ducked for cover.

Clint had his gun out, was trying to see where the shots were coming from. From the sound he figured one shooter, with a rifle. Buck had been a sitting duck, standing in the middle of the street like that, so Clint assumed that the shooter was missing on purpose.

Welcome to the neighborhood, he thought. Maybe somebody was just testing him to see what his reactions were.

A few minutes later he decided that was what was happening, because there were no further shots. He stood up carefully, looked over to where Buck was lying sprawled in the dirt. He waved and the deputy got up and walked over to him, gun in hand.

"What happened?" he asked. "What was that all about?"

"I don't know," Clint said, his eyes raking the rooftops across from them. "Buck, I want you to check behind those buildings."

"Sure, Sheriff," Buck said. "Uh, what am I lookin' for?"

"Anything you can find," Clint said. "Access to the rooftops, tracks in the dirt . . . anything you can, Buck—and be careful!"

"Yes, sir."

As Buck went to check the backs of the buildings, Clint approached them from the front. The hotel where he was staying was directly across from the office. Flanking it was a hardware store on one side, and a store on the other that sold ladies' clothing.

He checked the hotel first. As he entered, the desk clerk looked up at him.

"Um, Mr. Adams?" he said.

"Sheriff Adams for now," Clint said. "Anybody come through here in the past ten or fifteen minutes?"

"Uh, no, sir," the clerk said.

"Are you sure?"

"I've been here the whole time, sir," the clerk said. "I haven't seen anyone."

"Where's your roof access?"

"At the end of the hall from your room," the clerk said.

"Keep your eyes open," Clint said.

"For what?"

"Did you hear shots outside just now?"

"No, sir."

"Well, somebody took a couple of shots at me and my deputy," Clint said. "Just watch for anybody coming through here, maybe carrying a rifle."

"A rifle?"

"Don't worry," Clint said. "They won't hurt you. If you

see someone, just stay out of their way, but let me know which way they go."

"Uh, yes, sir."

"Oh, and tell me if you recognize who it is."

The clerk nodded.

Clint went up to the second floor and walked to the end of the hall. There was a hatch in the roof. He looked around, saw a couple of chairs that could have been used to climb up. What he didn't know was whether or not there was access from an adjoining roof, or somewhere else. He had to go up and find out.

He pulled a chair over, stepped up, and pushed open the hatch. He would have liked to climb up with his gun in his hand, but there was no way he could do that. He needed both hands to reach up and pull himself through.

He took a deep breath, pulled himself up and through the hatch, then quickly rolled aside and drew his gun. He came up on one knee and looked around. There was no one on the roof with him. He was alone.

He got to his feet, walked to both sides. Those building were too low to offer access, unless someone had a ladder. He didn't see one.

He walked to the front and looked down. There was no access there. On the street, people were just starting to move around again after the shooting.

He walked to the rear and looked down, saw Buck in the alley that ran along the backs of the buildings.

"See anything, Buck?"

"I think so," Buck said.

"Where?"

"On the ground behind the hardware store," Buck said. "Looks like somebody might've used a ladder."

"I'm coming down," Clint called. "Wait for me."

TWELVE

"You're right," Clint said. "There was a ladder set up here."

Clint stood up. Near the base of the building were the marks of a ladder in the dirt.

"So they took the shots from the roof of the hardware store?" Buck said.

"Or they pulled the ladder up behind them and then used it to get on the roof of the hotel."

"So they fired—what? Three shots? Then had to use the ladder to get down from both rooftops? That would have taken a while, wouldn't it?"

"We were on our bellies," Clint said. "Couldn't stand 'til we were sure the shooting was over. That gave whoever it was the time to climb down and get away."

"You wanna go up on the roof?" Buck asked. "I can go and find a ladder."

"No," Clint said. "I want to check the ground back here. Might be some tracks to follow."

They walked down the alley behind the building and Clint thought he could identify the tracks of the man with the ladder.

"How can you tell?" Buck asked.

"These tracks are right in front of where the ladder would have been," Clint said. "See that rundown heel?"

"Don't lots of men's boots have rundown heels?"

"Yes, they do. But we're going to follow this one anyway."

"Yes, sir."

They followed the tracks until they started to commingle with others in the dirt.

"I can't see 'em anymore," Buck said.

"We're behind the saloon," Clint said. "More foot traffic back here. Let's keep going."

They kept going and eventually found a ladder propped against the back of the building.

"Think this is the one?" Buck asked.

"It's long enough," Clint said. "What building is this?"

"I think it's the whorehouse," Buck said. "Miss Jean's."

"So it's either our ladder, or somebody's planning to elope with a whore," Clint said.

"Naaaw!" Buck said.

"Let's go inside."

In the front hall of the whorehouse, Clint was greeted by Miss Jean, a past-her-prime whore running her own house now. She was fifty or more, with lots of pancake makeup on her face and about thirty pounds more than she needed to pack on her five-two frame.

"You want to know what?" she asked.

"If anybody came in here in the past twenty minutes or so."

"Well . . . yeah," Miss Jean said. "A few men."

"Men you know?"

"I know most of the men in this town . . . except you," she said. "You the new sheriff? What happened to Jack Harper?"

"Jack got shot by the Graves gang," Clint said. "I'm taking his place until he can come back. Can we get back to those men? Regular customers?"

"Yeah."

"How many?"

"Three men, three regular customers," she said.

"Who are they?"

Miss Jean looked at Buck.

"Ya gotta tell him, ma'am," Buck said.

"Well . . . Ben Bratton."

Clint looked at Buck.

"Runs the Feed and Grain," Buck said. "He's fifty, weighs about three hundred pounds."

"Always chooses the smallest girl in the house," Miss Jean said. "Go figure."

"Can't see him using a ladder to get up on a roof," Clint said. "Who else?"

"Eric Young."

Again, Clint looked at Buck.

"Sixty or so," Buck said. "Does odd jobs. Married but tries to stay away from home as much as he can."

"Can't see him on a roof with a rifle," Clint said. "Who else?"

"Ben Manning."

"Don't think I know him," Buck said.

"He comes to town from the Crooked K Ranch to use a girl once in a while," she said, "but then he goes right back. He doesn't hang around town much."

"What's he look like?"

"Young," she said, "in his late twenties, kinda shy."

"Does he wear a gun?"

"Well, yeah."

"Didn't have a rifle with him when he got here, did he?"

"No."

"There's a ladder propped against the back of the house," Clint said. "You know anything about that?"

"We been havin' some work done on the roof," she said. "Must be the carpenter's."

"Somebody could have borrowed it and brought it back," Clint said.

"I wouldn't know," she said.

"I have to talk to this Ben Manning," Clint said.

"Can you wait until he's done?" she asked. "I don't want to scare my girls."

"I can wait for him, Sheriff," Buck said, "bring him over to you."

Clint was about to say no, but changed his mind. This might be a good test for Buck.

"Okay," he said. "Stay here. Miss Jean will point him out when he comes down and then you bring him to me."

"Yes, sir."

"No trouble, Buck."

"No, sir," Buck said. "I'll just bring 'im."

"Okay."

THIRTEEN

Clint went back to the office to wait for Buck to bring Ben Manning in. When the door opened, a young man looking the worse for wear entered, with Buck behind him. Clint assumed this was Ben Manning. He had a swelling under one eye that would soon turn black, and a bloody lip. He had an empty holster and Buck was carrying his gun.

"I thought I said no trouble, Buck," Clint said.

"I didn't start any trouble, Sheriff," Buck said. "He did. Didn't wanna come."

"You tell him all I wanted was to talk to him?" Clint asked.

"I told him," Buck said. "Still didn't wanna come, and took a swing at me."

"That so? Toss him in a cell—"

"Hey, wait," Manning said. "Look, I'm sorry, but if I'm late back to the ranch, I'll lose my job. You put me in a cell, I'll lose my job for sure."

"You should've thought of that before you took a swing at a lawman, Ben," Clint said.

"I know, I'm sorry," Manning said.

"Well . . . okay," Clint said. "If you answer some questions, maybe I'll just let you go back to the ranch."

"What kind of questions?"

Clint put his hand out for Buck to hand him Manning's gun. Clint sniffed it. Hadn't been fired in a while.

"Why you smellin' my gun?"

"Did you take a couple of shots at me a little while ago?" Clint asked.

"And one at me?" Buck added.

"What? Why would I wanna shoot at you?"

"Answer the question."

"No, I didn't take a shot at either one of you."

"Where's your horse?"

"At the livery."

"If I check your rifle, what will I find?"

"Ain't been fired."

"Buck."

"I'll walk over there and check it," Buck said, and left.

"Sit down," Clint said.

The young man pulled up a chair and sat down.

"Did you see a ladder leaning against the back of the whorehouse when you got there?"

"That ladder's been there for days."

"See a man with a rifle around there?"

"No."

"You know any reason why anybody would want to take a shot at me and Buck?"

"Hell, no."

"Do you know what happened to Sheriff Harper?"

"No."

"He was shot by the Graves gang," Clint said.

"That's too bad. Dead?"

"No."

"That's good."

"I'm taking his place until he's back on his feet. Do you know how to use a gun?"

Manning averted his eyes.

"No."

"That's a lie."

"Okay, so I can shoot," Manning said, "but I ain't fired either of my guns in a while."

"How long's a while?"

"Few months."

"How long you been working at the Crooked K?"

"A few months."

"So you haven't fired your gun since you started working there?"

"That's right."

"Why not?"

"Ain't had a reason to."

"Where'd you live before you came here?"

"Nowhere," Manning said. "I just . . . drifted."

"What made you decide to stop here?"

Manning shrugged.

"Got tired of driftin'."

"How long you plan on working there?"

"I don't know," Manning said, "but awhile longer anyway. That's why I don't wanna get fired."

At that point Buck reentered the room, carrying a rifle. He handed it to Clint.

"Ain't been fired that I can see," he said.

Clint sniffed the rifle, came to the same conclusion.

"This your rifle?" he asked Manning.

"Yeah."

Clint stared at the young man, then said, "Okay, you can go."

Manning stood up.

"Can I have my guns?"

"Sure."

Clint handed him the rifle and the handgun, which Manning holstered.

"I'm sorry I took a swing at you, Deputy," Manning said to Buck.

"That's okay."

Manning nodded, nodded again to Clint, and then left.

"You sure it wasn't him?" Buck asked.

"I'm sure."

"What do we do now?"

"Now," Clint said, "we go and get something go eat—and we watch our backs."

FOURTEEN

"There's something about Manning," Clint said.

"Like what?" Buck asked.

The deputy had taken Clint to a nearby café, which he said made good steaks. He was right.

"He didn't want to talk about guns," Clint said. "I get the feeling there's more to him than meets the eye."

"Like what?"

"I don't know, but he's hiding something. Who owns the Crooked K?"

"Feller named Ian Kennedy."

"And who runs it for him?"

"The foreman's name is Ed Michaels."

"What's Michaels like?"

A good ramrod," Buck said. "Tough."

"Young?"

Buck shook his head. "Old."

"Older than you?"

"Yeah."

"Younger than me?"

Buck hesitated.

"Go ahead," Clint said. "Say it."

"'Bout your age."

"Any men on that ranch who can shoot?"

"Maybe."

"Guess I should talk with Mr. Michaels."

"There's a feller in town you might want to talk to, also."

"Oh? Who?"

"His name's Minnesota."

"That's his name?"

Buck shrugged.

"First or last?"

Buck shrugged again.

"Why should I talk to him?"

"He can shoot."

"Have you seen him?"

"Once."

"Trick shooting?"

Buck shook his head.

"Two men drew down on him one day."

"What happened?"

"He killed 'em."

"Just like that?"

"Just like that."

"That happened here?"

Buck nodded.

"And Jack didn't arrest him?"

"It was a fair fight," Buck said. "In fact, they pushed him into it."

"Why?"

"They were makin' fun of him."

"Fun of him . . . how?"

"Well . . . he's kinda . . . little."

"Short, you mean?"

"Yeah."

"And sensitive about it?"

"Not sensitive, really . . . not unless you push him, I guess."

"Where is he?"

"Usually hangin' out at the Red Queen."

"Saloon?"

Buck nodded.

"Buck," Clint said, "we have to come to an agreement."

"About what?"

"When I ask you a question," Clint said, "I'm going to need more than a nod or a head shake from you. Understand?"

Buck nodded . . . then quickly said, "Yes, sir."

FIFTEEN

Clint locked the sheriff's office, told Buck to get a good night's sleep, then crossed the street to the hotel. He entered his room carefully, just in case the shooter from earlier in the day had found his way into his room.

There was a straight-backed wooden chair in the room. He locked the door, then lodged the chair beneath the doorknob. There was no access by the window, so he simply made sure it was locked.

That done, he undressed and got into bed. It had been a long day, things happening that he never would have expected. Being shot at, that was pretty much a common occurrence in his life, but the rest of the day had been odd, to say the least.

He'd never expected to come out of this day as the new town sheriff. But now that he was, he was going to do his damndest to make sure he had the shortest tenure of any sheriff in history.

Clint woke early the next morning to a persistent knocking at his door. He slid out of bed, grabbed his gun, and went to the door.

"Who is it?"

"Doc Foster. We're ready to move Sheriff Harper to the stage."

"I'll be right there, Doc," Clint said.

He dressed quickly and then hurried down the hall to Harper's room. The door was open and the room looked full of men.

"There you are," Foster said.

Clint entered the room, saw a wooden door lying on the floor.

"We're gonna move him to that door, facedown, and then carry him down."

Clint looked around, didn't recognize any of the men, but they all looked able enough.

"That you, Clint?" Harper yelled.

"I'm here, Jack."

"Make sure these jaspers don't drop me down the stairs," Harper said. "Doc says it might kill me."

"Don't worry, Jack," Clint said. "I'll shoot the first man who drops you."

The other men in the room widened their eyes.

"All right, then," Foster said. "Let's get movin'!"

They managed to carry Harper down the stairs without dropping him, and got him situated inside the stage, still on the door.

"Doc, how are you going to ride with him?" Clint asked.

"I'll squeeze in," the old sawbones said.

"Well, send me a telegram when the surgery's finished," Clint said. "Let me know how he comes through it."

"I'll do that," Foster said, squeezing into the stage.

Clint stuck his head in the window and said, "Good luck, Jack."

"Hey," Harper said, "I heard somebody took a shot at you last night."

"A couple of shots."

"That because you're wearin' my badge?"

"Could be," Clint said. "Could also be because of my reputation. You never know. Why don't you just worry about your surgery?"

"Hey, Clint."

"Yeah."

"If I don't come out of this alive—"

"Don't get sappy on me, Jack."

"No, I just wanna say . . . thanks."

"Okay," Clint said. "Okay."

Clint moved around to the front of the stage, climbed up to talk to the driver.

"You just have to remember one thing," Clint said.

"What's that?"

"If he dies on your stage, you'll have to answer to me. Got it?"

"Um, yeah, sure, Mr. Adams. I got it."

Clint climbed back down, went over to talk to Doc Foster.

"You got a gun, Doc?" he asked.

"Why would I need a gun?"

"You never know."

Doc held up his black bag and patted it.

"I've got one."

"Good."

Clint stepped away from the stage, looked up at the driver, and said, "Go!"

SIXTEEN

Later in the day Buck took Clint to the Red Queen to look for Minnesota.

The Red Queen was smaller than the Dust Cutter Saloon, with no gambling and no girls, just a bartender behind the bar and a few patrons.

"Is he here?" Clint asked.

"No," Buck said, "but he should be here soon."

"Let's have a beer, then," Clint said.

They went to the bar, told the bartender to ring two beers.

"Sure, Sheriff," the barman said.

He set two beers in front of them and then went back to doing nothing at the other end of the bar.

"Has Minnesota been in today?" Buck called out to him.

"Not yet," the man said, "but he'll be here. He always comes in here."

"That's what I said," Buck told Clint.

"I know," Clint said. "We'll wait."

"Okay, Clint."

They drank their beer in silence until Buck asked, "So you think the sheriff will be okay?"

"Sure," Clint said. "Sure. He's a strong man, and Doc

Foster said the doctors in Kansas City are real good. He'll be fine."

"You really think so?"

"Yes, Buck, I really think so."

"That's good," Buck said. "Real good."

Clint drank the rest of his beer and signaled the bartender for another one.

"What would you do if he didn't come back?" Buck asked.

"What?"

"If the sheriff doesn't come back," Buck said. "What would you do?"

"Well, Buck, I hope that when he does come back, I'll already be gone."

"Where?"

"I don't know," Clint said. "Just gone."

"But . . . who would be the sheriff, then?"

"I don't know . . . look, I told Jack I'd wear the badge until I found somebody else who could wear it."

"So . . . you're not stayin'?"

"No, I'm not staying."

"No, I mean, until the Graves gang comes back. You're stayin' until then, right?"

"Probably," Clint said. "I mean, it depends on when they come back. I expect that they'll come back sooner than later. I hope to get some men together before then, men who'll be able to stand up to them."

"But you'll be here, too, right? When they come back?" Buck asked.

"Probably."

"Clint—"

"Have another beer, Buck," Clint said, "and stop asking so many questions."

Miss Jean thought it was odd that such a small man would always choose a big woman.

"You sure you want Elspeth?" she asked Minnesota.

"I'm sure."

Elspeth was almost fat. She stood five foot nine and had mountainous breasts and buttocks. Miss Jean kept her around for big men who liked big girls, but even she looked down on this fellow.

"Okay," Miss Jean said. "Go on up to room five."

"Thanks."

She watched as he went up the stairs. She rarely talked with the girls about their clients, but Minnesota had been there several times now, and always chose a woman taller and larger than himself. She thought that this time she was going to ask Ellie what he had in that small package . . .

Minnesota knocked on the door, opened it, and stepped in. Elspeth was on the bed, already naked. He drank in the acres of flesh before him. Her huge breasts were tipped with large, pink nipples, and between her meaty, pale thighs was a forest of black hair.

"Minnesota," she said, "you cute thing. You came back to your Ellie? Last time you were with Diane."

"I like to spread it around, Ellie," he said, unstrapping his gun belt.

"Well, come on over here and spread it all over me, honey," she said.

Minnesota liked that Ellie was a big girl, but what he also liked was that she was young—younger than him. She had a beautiful face and the prettiest smooth skin. And she always smelled so good.

He got himself naked, and already his cock was rigid. Ellie—and the other girls—had been shocked to see what Minnesota was packing. He may have been small of stature, but there was nothing small about his penis.

He climbed on the bed with Ellie and let her enfold him in her arms, his face pressed between her breasts. He nursed on one big nipple, then the other, holding each breast in turn in both hands.

"You lie back, honey," she said, pushing him down. "Your Ellie wants to enjoy that big tallywacker of yours. Mmm." She slid down his body, kissing his chest, his belly, poking her tongue into his belly button. Finally, she was down between his legs, his big penis in both hands. She licked the head, wetting it, then smiled at him before taking him into her mouth.

"Oh, shit, girl!" he said as she took him all the way in.

Her head began to bob up and down as she sucked him, making wet noises, occasionally gagging on the size of him, but not letting him get the better of her. She wanted to prove she could handle the entire length and width of him. She liked Minnesota because he was a young, unscarred, and usually smelled better than most of the men who came to Miss Jean's.

With Minnesota, she could take as well as give pleasure . . .

Later, Minnesota was on his knees between her chunky legs, driving his cock into her while holding those legs open. Each time he slammed into her, ripples went through her breasts and belly.

"Oooh, baby, yeah, like that," she cooed to him. "Give it to me."

He didn't even care if she was just giving him whore talk. He knew he was giving it to her good, and that she liked it.

"Oh, baby, I like it just like that," she said, "but when you gonna flip me over, baby? I like when you do it to me from behind."

"Then flip on over, girl!" he told her.

He withdrew from her, his cock glistening with her juices. She rolled over and got to her knees, presenting her majestic butt to him. The cleavage between her cheeks was deep enough for him to fuck, and he did that for a while, like he had done earlier with her big tits. Finally, though, he spread those fleshy cheeks, pressed the head of his cock to her little brown anus, and pushed. She had taught him this, and said she didn't do it with any of her other clients.

He didn't care, as long as she did it with him.

When Minnesota came down the stairs, his legs were shaking. He had given it to Ellie good this time, but she had given as good as she got.

At the foot of the stairs Miss Ellie was waiting.

"Are you satisfied?" she asked.

"Oh yeah," he said, "I'm real satisfied. Now I need to get me a drink."

The odd thing about Minnesota—the other odd thing—was that after he was with one of the girls, he always seemed to be drunk. And yet she knew he wasn't because she didn't allow any liquor in her house. She had seen too many cowboys get liquored up in the past and hurt one of the girls. One time a girl even got her face cut up, which made her good for nothing but cleaning the house after that.

Minnesota gave Miss Jean a lopsided grin and said, "That gal, she's somethin' special."

"She sure is," Miss Jean. "One of my best."

"I'll be back."

I know you will, she thought as he went out the door. Then she went upstairs to ask Elspeth the question she'd been wondering about.

SEVENTEEN

"Is that him?"

Buck turned to look. The batwings had opened and a man entered. He was short—about five-five—and young. Clint figured him to be about twenty-five, probably two or three years younger than Buck Wilby.

"That's him," Buck said. "That's Minnesota."

"Beer, Jimmy!" Minnesota yelled, approaching the bar.

"Minnesota," Buck said.

The smaller man turned to look at him while the bartender set a beer in front of him.

"Hey, Deputy Buck," Minnesota said. "How're ya doin'?"

"Good, Minnesota. I want you to meet the new sheriff," Buck said. "This is Clint Adams."

"New sheriff?" Minnesota said. "What new sheriff? Where's Sheriff Harper?"

"The sheriff was shot when the Graves gang tried to rob the bank," Clint said. "He's gone to Kansas City to have surgery."

"Well, that's too bad."

Minnesota was dressed in trail clothes that were rather worn, a denim jacket with frayed elbows, but the peacemaker in his holster was well cared for.

"Well, it's good to meet ya," Minnesota said. "Buck said your name was . . ."

"Clint Adams."

"Adams," Minnesota said. "Clint . . . Adams?"

"That's right."

The younger man drank some beer, then frowned at Clint and asked, "Clint Adams? The Gunsmith?"

"That's right," Buck said.

"And you're the sheriff?"

"That's right."

"Well," Minnesota exclaimed, "whataya know? Jimmy, beers all around. We're celebratin' the new sheriff."

The bartender set up three beers.

"Minnesota," Buck said, "the sheriff wants to talk to you."

"He does? About what?"

"I guess I better let him tell you that," Buck said.

"Let's take our beers to that back table," Clint said. "That okay with you, Minnesota?"

"It's fine with me, Sheriff Adams," Minnesota said. "Just fine!"

It became apparent to Clint that Minnesota had been drinking before he got to the Red Queen. But he seemed to be able to hold his liquor fairly well. Still, Clint wanted to talk to him before he had any more to drink.

"You didn't hear about the bank robbery?" Clint asked. "About the sheriff shooting it out with the Graves boys?"

"No," Minnesota said, "I was outta town. What's the big deal? The sheriff stopped them and he's gonna be all right, right?"

"Well," Clint said, "we have to wait and see what happens after the surgery. He was shot twice in the back, and the bullets are close to his spine."

"That's too bad."

"But the other thing, the reason he asked me to wear the badge, is that the Graves gang is going to be coming back, and with more men."

"Really? When?"

"We're not sure," Clint said, "but I want to try and get some men together to face them with me and Buck."

"Deputies?"

"Well, not really deputies. Just men from town, who have an interest in protecting it."

"So, like a posse, but in town."

"Right."

Minnesota sat back and laughed.

"What's so funny?" Buck asked.

"You're gonna have a hard time with that," the younger man said.

"Why?" Buck asked.

"The men in this town ain't gonna want to face up to a gang like that," Minnesota said. "Not these fine folks— storekeepers, politicians, and the like."

"If they don't," Clint said, "the Graves gang might burn the town to the ground."

"Well, that ain't gonna happen either, is it?" Minnesota asked.

"Why not?" Clint asked.

"Because you're gonna stop 'em," Minnesota said. "You're the Gunsmith, and you're the law. You and Buck. It's your job."

"Well," Clint said, "you may be right about that, but I think we're going to need some help."

"Wait a minute," Minnesota said. "You're gonna ask me?"

"You're the first one we're asking," Clint said.

"Why?" Minnesota asked. "Why me?"

"I understand you know your way around a gun," Clint said.

"Where'd you hear that?"

Minnesota suddenly seemed completely sober, and Clint now had second thoughts about him being drunk when he got there. The young man looked over at Buck accusingly.

"What?" Buck said. "I just told him what I saw that time."

"Buck tells me you took two men in a fair fight," Clint said.

"Maybe they weren't so much," Minnesota offered.

"And maybe you're just pretty good with a gun," Clint said. "Why would you deny that?"

"I didn't deny nothin'," Minnesota said. He took a moment to drink some beer.

"Well, see, here, I need men who can handle a gun," Clint said.

Minnesota sat back and looked at Clint.

"Okay," he said, "you payin'?"

"Probably regular posse rates."

"A dollar a day?"

"It's your town, too, Minnesota—"

"Actually, it ain't," Minnesota said. "I ain't from here."

"Well," Buck said, "nobody's really from here—"

"Me less than anybody," Minnesota said.

"Where are you from?" Clint asked. "Minnesota?"

"That don't matter," the other man said. "Look, I got no stake in this fight, and a dollar a day just ain't gonna do it. If you want me, you're gonna have to pay."

"Well," Clint said, "if I'm going to pay, I'd like to see what I'm getting."

"What, you want a demonstration?"

"I need something."

"You want me to shoot a cigarette out of the bartender's mouth?"

"I don't need a trickshooter, Minnesota," Clint said, "I need a man who can shoot at somebody while they're shooting back. But that takes a special kind of man. Maybe I just ought to forget about it—"

"Not so fast, Sheriff. You already know what I can do . . ." Minnesota said. "Why don't you let me think about this for a while, Sheriff?"

"Okay, Minnesota," Clint said, pushing his chair back, "but don't take too long, okay? This town might just get burned down around our ears."

EIGHTEEN

Frank Graves sat at a table in the Silver Star Saloon, his left leg straight out to try and ease the pain from the bullet wound. The bullet had been put there by the sheriff of Guardian, Missouri, Jack Harper, when Harper broke up their bank job. But Graves and his brother, Dudley, had repaid Harper with two bullets in his back.

"Sammy!" he called.

Sammy Holt turned and looked at Graves. Holt was a young man, a new member of the gang, and as such he usually ended up running Frank Graves's errands.

"Yeah, Frank?" Holt asked from the bar.

"Bring me another beer."

"Comin' up, boss," Holt said.

The young man came running over with the beer and put it down in front of Graves.

"You know where Dudley is?" Graves asked.

"Whorehouse, I think."

"Get 'im."

"Interrupt him?"

"That's what I said."

"Um, he won't like it, boss."

"You tell him I sent you," Graves said. "If he kills you, I'll make sure he apologizes."

"Um . . . sure." Holt swallowed hard, then left the saloon to find Dudley Graves.

Dudley Graves was enjoying two women in the whorehouse when there was a timid knock on the door of the room.

"What the hell—" he said.

The two girls—a skinny redhead and an older, heavier brunette—rolled away from him. They knew what happened when Dudley got mad. He swung at whatever or whoever was closest to him.

Dudley got to his feet and lumbered to the door. He was naked, his sloppy belly hanging down so that it almost hid his rigid penis. He grabbed his gun from the foot of the bed on the way. When he opened the door, he pointed the gun.

"Jeez, Dudley!" Sammy Holt said.

"Gimme one good reason why I shouldn't blow your head off!" Dudley said.

"Frank sent me to get you."

"He know where I am?"

"Yeah, he does."

"Then he knows what I'm doin'."

"Yes."

"And he still sent you to interrupt me?"

"Um, y-yeah."

Dudley lowered the gun.

"Must be important, then."

He turned from the door, walked to the bed, and started getting dressed.

Standing in the doorway, Holt wanted to avert his eyes rather than look at Dudley's sloppy nakedness. But there were also two naked women in the room. So he stared at them. They smiled and made faces at him.

Dressed, Dudley buckled his gun belt and holstered his gun, then looked at the girls on the bed.

"Sorry, gals, no Dudley today."

The girls contrived to look disappointed, even though they were glad they weren't going to have to service the big man.

"What about him?" the redhead asked, pointing at Sammy Holt.

"Him? He ain't never had a woman before," Dudley said. He looked at Holt. "You ever been with a woman, boy?"

"S-Sure."

"You lie!" Dudley said. He looked at the girls again. "He's a virgin. What would you want with him?"

"We could teach him a thing or two," the brunette said.

"You paid for our time already," the redhead said.

"Well, that's true," Dudley said. "And I wouldn't want you to be totally disappointed." He looked at Holt again. "Whataya say, boy? You want two girls?"

"Um . . ." Holt said nervously.

Dudley grabbed him by the front of the shirt and pulled him into the room.

"He's all yours, girls," he said. "Do what you want with him."

"Dud—" Holt started.

"My brother say he wanted to see you, or me?" Dudley asked.

"Well, you—"

"Be gentle with him, girls," Dudley said. "Boy, you're in for a treat, and it's on me."

Dudley left the room, slamming the door behind him.

Holt turned and looked at the two naked girls. The redhead had small breasts, but her nipples were very large. On the other hand, the brunette had chubby breasts with small, brown nipples. Staring at Holt, she spread her legs and ran her fingers through her dark pubic hair. When he looked at the redhead again, she was stroking herself, making herself wet. He could smell her.

"Um, I'm, uh, not like Dudley," he told them.

"That's good," the redhead said.

"He's awful," the brunette said.

"A brute."

"And he smells," the brunette added.

"And he's no good in bed," the redhead said. "He thinks he is, but he's not. And he's . . . small."

"What? He's a huge man."

The girls laughed.

"Not where it counts," the redhead said.

"Oooh, look at his pants," the brunette said. "How about takin' off your clothes, boy?"

"I ain't a boy," Holt said.

"What's your name?" the redhead asked. She was closer to his age.

"Sammy."

"I'm Belinda," she said, "this is Mary. Take off your pants, Sammy. They're gettin' tight."

"Look," he said, "I never, I mean, I ain't ever—"

"Don't worry," the brunette said, getting off the bed, "we'll take care of it."

"We'll take care of everythin'," Belinda said.

She got off the bed and together the two girls undressed Holt until he was standing there naked. He tried to cover his crotch with his hands, but they pushed his hands away.

"Don't cover that up, Sammy," Mary said.

"Oh, my," Belinda said. "That's impressive."

"Really?" Holt stopped trying to cover his erection.

"It's pretty," Belinda said, touching him lightly. He jumped from her touch.

"Mmm, and he's clean," Belinda said, "and he has nice young skin."

Mary kissed his belly, ran her hands around behind him to stroke his buttocks.

Belinda began to stoke his penis with one hand, then leaned forward and kissed the tip. Sammy Holt gasped.

"This is gonna be fun," Belinda told Mary.

From behind Holt, her hands still on his ass, Mary peeked around at Belinda and said, "It sure is."

She reached up between his legs and cupped his sack while Belinda suddenly took his penis into her mouth.

"Jesus!" Holt gasped.

NINETEEN

Dudley Graves entered the saloon, spotted his brother sitting with half a beer. He went to the bar, got two more, and carried them to the table.

"How's the leg?" he asked, pushing a fresh beer across the table.

"Awful. Where's the kid?"

"I left him with the whores," Dudley said.

"What for?"

"Make a man out of him."

"Where are the others?"

"Around town."

"Come on, Dudley."

"We got two cousins playin' poker, one shootin' pool, one playin' horseshoes. We got one brother sleepin', one playin' poker, and Del is . . . well, I don't know where Del is."

"And the rest of the men?"

"I don't keep such good track of the nonrelatives," Dudley said. "Except Sammy."

"And he's with your whores."

"That's right."

"Ain't like you to share your women, Dud," Frank said.

"Hell, I paid for 'em already."

"You coulda got your money back."

Dudley stared a moment, then said, "I never thought of that."

Frank finished his beer and started on the fresh one his brother had brought him.

"What'd you wanna see me about?"

"I wanna go and take care of Guardian."

"Where?"

"Stupid," Frank said, "the town where we shot the sheriff."

"And he shot you," Dudley said. "And killed Mack."

Mack Reynolds had been riding with them, and the sheriff in Guardian had not only shot Frank in the leg, but killed Mack.

"We gotta go back there, get our money outta that bank, and take care of that town," Frank said.

"So when do we go?" Dudley asked. "You can't ride with that leg yet."

"It's gettin' better," Frank said. "It'll be healed soon."

"Still be stiff, though."

"That don't matter," Frank said. "Once I know that ridin' a horse won't make me bleed to death, we're goin' back there."

"They might have a new lawman by now."

"It don't matter," Frank said. "If they do have a new sheriff, then he'll have to pay for what the old one did."

"Suits me," Dudley said. "Nothin' I like more than killin' lawmen."

"I'll need you to round up Del, Hap, and Clell," Frank said, speaking of their brothers, "and the cousins. Let them know what we're plannin' on doin'."

"When do ya want me to do that?"

"Today."

"So soon? You ain't gonna be ready for a while yet—" Dudley started to argue, but Frank cut him off.

"I don't want anybody makin' any other plans," he said. "I want them all to know what we're plannin'."

"You know," Dudley said, "as the older brother, I should probably be the one doin' the plannin'."

"You're right, Dudley," Frank said, "you are the older brother. But I'm the smarter one, so I'm makin' the decisions."

Dudley fell silent for a few moments, then said, "Well, you don't mind if I finish my beer first, do ya?"

TWENTY

At the end of one week Clint had convinced Minnesota to join him and Buck, but the young man wanted a badge.

"You can hire everybody else for a dollar a day," he said, "but I wanna be a deputy, with a deputy's pay."

"Ain't much better," Buck had told him.

"It's a status thing," Minnesota said with a smile.

Clint agreed and made Minnesota a deputy.

Also at the end of that time they knew that Jack Harper had had his surgery, and had come through alive. What they didn't know was if he would walk again. Doc Foster's telegram said it would take some time after the surgery before they knew.

"Will keep you informed," the telegram ended.

Clint checked with the telegraph office each day at ten, when they had been open an hour.

Clint entered the sheriff's office, found both deputies there, drinking coffee.

"No word, today?" Buck asked.

"No."

He walked to the stove and poured himself some coffee, then turned and walked to the desk.

"When are we gonna get some more men?" Minnesota asked.

Clint looked at Buck.

"I got a couple of suggestions, but that's it," the deputy said.

"What about you, Minnesota?" Clint asked. "You know anybody?"

Minnesota shrugged.

"I don't know too many men in town, and the ones I do wouldn't help us. And I mean, even if they were willin', they wouldn't be any help."

"Well," Clint said, "nobody said all the help had to come from town."

"Why didn't you tell me that before?" Minnesota asked him.

"It makes a difference?" Clint asked.

"Hell, it makes a big difference. I know a couple of good boys, but they're in a town called Sensible."

"What?" Buck asked.

"Yeah," Minnesota said, "the town is actually called Sensible."

"Why not?" Clint said to Buck. "I know two other towns called Normal and Peculiar." He looked at Minnesota. "Is there a telegraph there?"

"No," Minnesota said. "If you want them, you'll have to go and get them."

Clint stood up.

"Then let's go ask them."

"What about the Graves gang?" Minnesota asked. "They might show up while we're gone."

"How far is Sensible?"

"Half a day."

"Graves isn't going to come back until he heals," Clint said. "Harper said he hit him in the leg. He also has to round up the rest of his family. I think we can spare one more day."

"What about me?" Buck asked.

"You stay here, Buck. We'll be back sometime after midnight. Talk to your boys and see if you can get them interested."

"We gonna ride at night?" Minnesota asked.

"We are," Clint said. "I only want to be gone one day."

"Well, then, we better get goin'," Minnesota said.

As they went out the front door, Clint called back to Buck, "Hold the fort!"

TWENTY-ONE

Half a day's ride brought them into the town of Sensible by dark. They left their horses in the livery but told the livery-man not to bed them down. Then they walked down the main street—one of two streets the town had.

"Small place," Clint said. "What are your friends doing here?"

"Just laying low."

"Who are these guys?"

"Their names are Wilkes and Commons," Minnesota said.

"First names or last names?"

"Only names."

"Like Minnesota?"

"Exactly."

"Where'd you get that name anyway?"

"What's wrong with it?" Minnesota said. "I like the name."

"There's nothing wrong with it," Clint said. "It's just a little . . . unusual."

"I picked it myself," Minnesota said.

"What was your name before that?"

Minnesota looked at Clint.

"If I wanted anybody to know that, I wouldn'ta picked a new name, would I?"

"Okay," Clint said. "Okay."

They walked up to the only saloon Clint could see.

"If they're still here," Minnesota said, "they'll be in there."

"You mean we rode all the way here and they might not be here?"

Minnesota shrugged.

"They might already have a job."

"What do they hire out to do?" Clint asked.

"Anything they can."

They entered the saloon, found it quiet, almost empty. No girls, no gaming tables. Almost no customers, except for two men sitting at separate tables.

"That's them," Minnesota said.

"Sitting at separate tables?"

Minnesota shrugged.

"They don't like each other."

"But they work together?"

"They work together real well," Minnesota said, "but they don't like each other. I can't figure it out, but it works for them."

"So what do we do?"

"We talk to them, one at a time," Minnesota said.

"Okay."

Clint started forward, but Minnesota put out his hand to stop him.

"Gotta buy them a beer."

Clint walked to the bar, bought three beers, and handed one to Minnesota.

"Okay," the smaller man said.

They approached the man sitting to their left, leaving the man on the right for later.

"Hey, Wilkes," Minnesota said.

The man looked up at them. He had a face that looked as if it had spent more than a few rounds in the ring. A scar split his left eyebrow right in half. His shoulders were broad, his arms thick with muscle. He looked around thirty-five.

"Minnesota," he said in a deep voice. "Whataya say?"

"Meet a friend of mine," Minnesota said. "Clint Adams."

Wilkes looked at Clint, who put the beer in front of him.

"Your friend's got a name I recognize, but he's wearin' a badge."

"He's not here lookin' for you behind a badge," Minnesota said. "Well, yeah, he is, but he wants your help."

"My help," Wilkes said. "With what?"

"Can we sit?" Clint asked.

"Sure," Wilkes said. "Why not?"

Clint and Minnesota pulled out chairs, sat down, and put their beers on the table.

Clint explained the situation—Harper getting shot stopping a bank robbery and the Graves gang planning to come back and finish the job.

"Graves," Wilkes said. "I heard of them. Family, right? Brothers? Cousins?"

"That's them."

"And you want my help stoppin' them?"

"That's right."

"What's in it for me?"

"I'll get you paid," Clint said. "I don't know how much yet."

"More than Minnesota's makin' as a deputy?" Wilkes asked.

"Probably."

"I tell you what," Wilkes said. "You talk to Commons over there. If he agrees to go, I'll agree to go."

"Okay," Clint said, "we'll talk to your friend—"

"He ain't no friend of mine!" Wilkes snapped.

"Sorry."

"We just work together," Wilkes said, "and if he says it's okay, I'll do it."

"All right," Clint said, standing up. "We'll talk to him."

Wilkes sipped his beer, then looked up at Clint.

"Gonna take more than a beer to get him to talk to you."

"Like what?" Clint asked.

"Like a bottle."

"Okay," Clint said, "a bottle it is."

"Good luck," Wilkes said. "He ain't in as good a mood as I am."

"I guess we'll have to see how persuasive I can be," Clint said.

He and Minnesota walked to the bar and collected a bottle of whiskey from the bartender.

"You ain't gonna bust up my place, are ya?" the barman asked.

"Why would we do that?" Clint asked.

"I don't know," he said. "Those two do it almost every night."

"How?"

"Fightin'."

"With who?"

The bartender shrugged.

"With each other," he said, "or whoever tries to get between 'em."

"Don't worry," Clint said. "We're not here to fight with them, or get between them."

"Yeah," Minnesota said, "we're just here to drink with 'em."

Clint started away from the bar, then turned back.

"You got law here?"

"No," the bartender said. "We only got about twenty-two people livin' here. Don't need no law. We take care of ourselves."

"Okay," Clint said, "whatever works for you, I guess."

"If you was to take those two out of here," the bartender said, "it'd be a lot quieter, though. A lot quieter."

"They seem pretty quiet," Clint said.

"Yeah," the bartender said, "now."

TWENTY-TWO

Minnesota and Clint carried their beers and the bottle over to the other table. The man called Commons had his head down on his crossed arms.

"Commons," Minnesota said.

The man didn't stir.

"Commons," Minnesota said, again, "we got whiskey."

Commons lifted his head. His eyes surprised Clint. They were bright blue, and clear. He hadn't been sleeping, and he wasn't drunk.

Clint put the bottle on the table, with a shot glass over the top.

"Hello, Minnesota," Commons said. "What the hell is that thing on your chest?"

"A badge," Minnesota said. "I'm a deputy."

"And who's your friend?"

"He's the sheriff of a town called Guardian."

"Stupid name for a town."

"That from a man sitting in a town called Sensible?" Clint asked.

Commons looked at him.

"What's your name?"

"Clint Adams."

"The Gunsmith?"

"That's right."

"Hell," Commons said, grabbing the bottle and removing the glass. "Siddown. I'll drink with the Gunsmith."

Clint and Minnesota sat down while Commons poured himself a drink.

"What can I do for you, Sheriff Clint Adams, the Gunsmith?"

"I've got an offer for you," Clint said.

"Well, let me have it, then."

Clint told his story for the second time in twenty minutes. Commons drank while he listened.

"So that's it," Clint said. "I've got a town to save and I need help doing it."

"Not enough men in your town to do it?" Commons asked.

"Not enough men who can handle a gun," Clint said, "and are willing to risk it."

"So you want me to risk my life when the people who live there won't?"

"That's about the size of it."

"And you asked Wilkes the same thing?"

"Yes."

"And what did he say?"

"He said he'll do it if you do it."

"He said that?"

"Yeah," Minnesota said, "he did."

Commons looked annoyed.

"That sonofabitch," he muttered. "Can't never make a decision for himself."

"I think he made a decision," Clint said.

"How's that?" Commons asked.

"He made a decision to go with your decision," Clint said. "I guess he must trust you."

Commons stared up at Clint, then poured another drink and downed it.

"Yeah, okay," he said.

"You'll do it?"

Commons nodded.

"We'll both do it," Commons said. "Hell, we got nothin' else to do but sit around this lousy little saloon in this lousy little town."

"Okay," Clint said. "Minnesota and I are heading back tonight."

"We'll be along," Commons said.

"When?"

"Tomorrow. Don't worry, Sheriff, we'll be along."

"Okay."

Clint and Minnesota stood up.

"One thing," Commons said.

"What's that?"

"We ain't wearin' no badges."

"That's okay," Clint said. "I don't have any more badges anyway."

TWENTY-THREE

Clint and Minnesota took their horses to the livery in Guardian, where they rubbed and bedded them down.

"I'm turnin' in," Minnesota said.

"I'll be at the office," Clint said. "Probably catch some sleep in one of the cells."

"You gonna check with Buck?" Minnesota asked. "See if he got anybody?"

"Yup."

Minnesota yawned.

"Well, let me know what he says."

They left the livery, walked together to the center of town, then split up. Minnesota went to the hotel, where Clint had gotten him a room. Clint walked over to the sheriff's office. When he walked in, Buck sat straight up in his chair, his feet falling off the sheriff's desk.

"Oh, Sheriff," Buck said.

"What are you doing here so late, Buck?"

"I'm in charge," Buck said. "Thought I'd stay in the office."

"Well, go get some sleep."

Buck stood up, rubbing his face with his hands.

"You just get back?"

"Yep."

"Get those men?"

"Yeah, names are Wilkes and Commons," Clint said. "They'll be here sometime after sunup"

"Any good?"

"Minnesota says they are," Clint said, "and you recommended him."

Buck headed for the door.

"What about you?" Clint asked.

Buck turned.

"You sign anybody up?"

"Two men," Buck said. "They're brothers, which is why I think they took the job."

"What are their names?"

"Harley and James Prescott," Buck said.

"Any good?"

"They've ridden on some posses with me and Sheriff Harper," Buck said. "They do what they're told, know how to use their guns."

"What do they do normally?"

"Odd jobs," Buck said. "Just odd jobs."

"Well," Clint said, "this is an odd job."

Buck stood there, nodding.

"Okay, Buck," Clint said. "Go get some sleep. When you wake up, bring the Prescott boys over here for me to meet."

"Okay, Sheriff."

Wilkes and Commons spoke very little until they rode into Guardian.

"At least it's a real town," Wilkes said. "More than one saloon, probably more than one whorehouse."

"More important," Commons said, "more than one place to eat."

"You got that right."

They rode to the livery, where they turned their horses over to the liveryman.

"How long?" the man asked.

"Until the Graves boys have come and gone," Commons said.

They walked away from the livery, heading toward the center of town.

"Now what?" Wilkes asked.

"Sheriff's office," Commons said. "Clint Adams should have someplace for us to stay."

"Maybe even an advance on our pay," Wilkes said.

"Don't go getting in trouble, Wilkes."

"I won't," the other man said, "not yet anyway."

TWENTY-FOUR

Later in the day Clint was in the office with Buck, Minnesota, Commons, Wilkes, and the Prescott brothers.

"This is it?" Commons asked. "Just the six of us?"

"So far," Clint said.

"How many men we facin'?" Wilkes asked.

"We're not sure," Clint said. "We know there's four or five brothers, and a bunch of cousins. They'll also have other gang members."

"So a dozen, or more?" Commons asked.

"Maybe."

"Buck told us you ain't gonna stop lookin' for men," Harley Prescott said.

"I'm not," Clint said, "but starting today we'll all have jobs to do."

"Like what?" Wilkes asked.

"Somebody will be on watch at all times. If you see a gang of men approaching town, you'll sound the alarm."

"Then what will we do?" James Prescott asked.

"We're going to work that out," Clint said. "I'll come up with a schedule, and we'll all have jobs. We'll rotate, too, so nobody does the same job day after day until the Graves gang gets here."

"Okay," Commons asked, "so what're our jobs?"

"I'll let you know later this evening," Clint said. "I'm going to work it all out. Meanwhile, get yourselves scheduled, get yourselves armed. Wilkes, get yourself a gun."

"I don't use a gun," Wilkes said.

"You own a rifle?"

"No."

"We'll get you one," Clint said. "You're not going to be able to use a knife, or your hands, when the Graves gang rides in."

"I don't use—"

"We'll get him a rifle," Commons said.

Wilkes looked at his partner, who just shook his head. The big man subsided.

"You boys make sure your guns are cleaned and in proper working order," Clint told the Prescotts. "Buck tells me you can shoot. I'll have to trust him."

"We can shoot," Harley Prescott said. "Rifles better than pistols, though."

"That's okay," Clint said. "My guess is we'll be doing a lot of rifle work when the time comes."

Clint was sitting on the edge of his desk while he talked. Now he stood up.

"That's all," Clint said. "Come back here tonight at seven, after you've all had supper."

"Suits me," Wilkes said. "I'm hungry now."

"Listen up," Clint said as the new recruits headed for the door.

They all stopped and turned.

"Prescotts, you fellas have your rooms already. Commons and Wilkes, I got you rooms at the hotel. But as far as meals go, you pay your way, understand? No free rides just because you're working for me."

"Sure, Sheriff," Harley said.

"No problem," James said.

Clint looked at Commons and Wilkes.

"Okay," Commons said.

Wilkes didn't say anything.

"Wilkes?" Clint said.

"Yeah," Wilkes said, "yeah, okay. No free rides. Can we go now?"

"You can go," Clint said. "Wilkes, if you want a gun, I will get you one for free. That okay with you?"

"That's fine," Wilkes said.

"Okay, then," Clint said. "See you all at seven."

The four recruits left. Clint turned to Buck and Minnesota.

"That okay with you fellas?"

"Sure, Sheriff," Buck said.

"Minnesota?"

"Strikes me you still ain't seen me shoot, Sheriff," Minnesota said.

"I have a feeling you'll hold your own," Clint said.

"That's so?"

"If we have a chance, though," Clint said, "I'll watch you shoot. In fact, I can watch all of you shoot. I'll try to work it out."

"Good," Minnesota said. "I'd like to see those Prescott boys shoot."

"And I'd like to see Commons and Wilkes shoot," Buck said.

"Wilkes usually likes to use his hands, or a knife," Minnesota said. "I don't think I've ever seen him fire a gun."

"That's okay," Clint said. "By the time the Graves gang gets here, he can learn."

Before any of them could say another word, the door to the office opened and Lucy Dennison came in.

"Oh, Sheriff," she said, "am I interrupting?"

"Not at all, Mrs. Dennison," Clint said. "Boys, I'll see you later."

"Sure, Sheriff," Minnesota said. "Come on, Buck, I'll buy you a drink."

The two deputies left.

TWENTY-FIVE

"What can I do for you, Mrs. Dennison?" Clint asked.

"I thought we settled on you calling me Lucy?" she said.

"Oh, right," he said. "Lucy."

"I think you promised me some supper last time we talked, and I haven't heard from you at all."

"Well, I'm, sorry, Lucy, but I have been a little busy. I've been meaning to come and see you."

"So I saved you the trouble," she said. "I've come to see you."

"It's a little early for supper," he said, "but I can meet you later—"

"No, no," she said, "that's not good enough. You'll promise to come and see me, and then you'll get busy again."

"Well, my job—"

"You're not doing anything right now, are you?" she asked.

"Um, not at this exact moment, no . . ." he said.

"So, there's no time like the present."

"For supper?"

"No," she said. She walked to the door, pulled the shade down over the window, and then locked the door. "Not supper." She turned to face him, her back to the door. She was wearing a skirt and a shirt, and she slowly unbuttoned the shirt and peeled it off. Underneath was a frilly black top.

"Lucy—"

"I think we should just skip the supper and get right to something else."

She undid her skirt and let it drop to the floor. Now all she was wearing was some black lace.

"I knew we'd end up like this the moment you walked into the Town Council meeting," she said. "I swore all the men in that room would be able to smell me, because I got so excited I became wet. But since they're all dried-up politicians, they didn't sense it. But you did, didn't you?"

"Well, uh—" He really hadn't, but he sure was sensing it now, wasn't he?

"Come here, Sheriff Adams," she said, crooking her finger at him. "Let's get better acquainted."

Buck and Minnesota went to the Red Queen Saloon and ordered a couple of beers.

"Who was the woman?" Minnesota asked.

"Mrs. Dennison," Buck said. "Her husband was on the Town Council until he died. Now she took his place."

"A woman on the Council?"

"I know," Buck said, "the men on the Council don't like it, but they have to wait for her husband's term to be over to get rid of her."

"Well, sure didn't look like the sheriff wanted to get rid of her, did it?"

"That lady?" Buck asked. "She's a little old, ain't she?"

"Son," Minnesota said, even though Buck was older, "ain't you ever been with an older woman?"

"Um, well, no . . ."

"Well," Minnesota said. "There ain't nothin' like bein' with an experienced woman—that is, 'less you're with a big woman."

"Big woman?"

"Big teats, big hips," Minnesota said dreamily. "Nothin' like 'em. In fact, I think I'm gonna finish this beer and head over to Miss Jean's."

"The whorehouse?"

"Ain't you ever been there?"

"Um, no."

"Aw, come on, son," Minnesota said. "Drink up and I'll take you over there. We got nothin' to do 'til supper anyway."

"Well . . . okay."

"Drink up," Minnesota said, slapping Buck on the back. "You're gonna love it!"

"Lucy," Clint said, "you're a beautiful woman, but this isn't the time or place—"

"Don't tell me that," she said, staring down at his crotch. "You can't tell me you're not excited at the prospect of having sex in jail."

"In jail?"

"In one of your cells," she said.

"Lucy—"

"This ties in the back," she said, stepping away from the door and reaching behind her. "All I have to do is pull and . . . oops."

TWENTY-SIX

Frank Graves flexed his right leg again and again, flinching at the pain. He was sitting in a wooden chair in front of the hotel.

"How's it feel?" Dudley asked, coming out the door.

"Better," Frank said.

"Ready to ride?"

"A couple more days," Frank said. "Let everybody know. Two days."

"And then two days' ride to Guardian," Dudley said. "So in four days we burn that town to the ground."

"After we hit the bank."

"Why do the rest of you go through your money so fast?" the big man asked.

"Because we spend it on more than whores," Frank said.

"Speaking of which," Dudley said, "the kid's over at the whorehouse again."

"That can't be," Frank said. "He got no money left. He spent it all."

"I loaned him some."

"What for?"

"He's a new man, Frank," Dudley said. "Them whores love him."

"Why?"

"Beats me," Dudley said. "I think it's because he's so young."

"That must be it," Frank said. "You find Del?"

"Not yet."

"Well, what the hell—"

"You know Del," Dudley said.

"Yeah, I know him," Frank said, "and I want you to make sure he's not in jail, or in any kind of trouble."

"Why me?"

"Because you know how to handle him," Frank said. "You're the big brother."

"Oh, now I'm the big brother?" Dudley said. "I thought you were in charge."

"I am in charge," Frank said. "That's why I'm tellin' you to find Del, and if he's in trouble, you get him out. We need him for this job."

"Okay," Dudley said. "I'll go get 'im."

"And haul that kid out of the whorehouse," Frank said. "He's gonna wear it down to the nub."

"Ha," Dudley said. "He probably started out that way."

When the Prescotts left the sheriff's office, Wilkes asked them which was the best saloon in town.

"The Dust Cutter," Harley said.

"That's where we're goin' now," James said.

"I'll tag along," Wilkes said. "What about you, Commons?"

"Sure, why not?" Commons said. "I don't know anybody else in town. But remember, the sheriff said to stay out of trouble."

"And I told him I would."

When they got to the saloon, they went right to the bar and ordered four beers.

Wilkes turned with a mug in his hand and looked at the girls working the floor.

"Look, Commons, a real saloon with real girls," Wilkes said.

"Real saloon girls are what get you into trouble, Wilkes," Commons said. "Just drink your beer, look at them, and be satisfied with that."

"He likes girls?" Harley asked.

"Saloon girls?" James asked.

"He likes girls, but he don't know what to do with them," Commons said, keeping his voice low. "Then he gets mad, and he gets into fights."

"He's a pretty big guy," James said.

"Yeah," Commons said, "runs about six-four, and he's pretty strong. In fact, he's the strongest man I ever met."

"You know," Harley said, "I hear Dudley Graves is pretty strong."

"One of them Graves boy?" Commons asked.

"The oldest one."

"So you know these fellas who rob banks and shoot sheriffs?"

"We heard of 'em," James said. "But we don't know 'em."

"Not personally," Harley said.

"Well, I'll bet Wilkes is stronger than Dudley Graves," Commons said.

"You and him been friends a long time?" Harley asked.

"Oh, we ain't friends," Commons said. "We just work together."

"Oh," James said.

"I got better taste than to be friends with him," Commons said, and turned to lean on the bar.

TWENTY-SEVEN

Lucy stood in front of the locked door, totally naked. She took Clint's breath away. He never would have expected her body to look like that. Heavy breasts—the way he had come to like them—pale, smooth skin, a pubic thatch that was black and bushy—something else he liked.

"One of us is overdressed," she said.

Clint undid his gun belt and put it on the desk, then undressed, beginning with his boots. When he was naked, he turned to face Lucy, who caught her breath.

"Oh, my . . ." she said.

He walked to her and took her in his arms, trapping his hard column of flesh between them. As they kissed, he slid his hands around to cup her buttocks and they began to grind their crotches together.

He lifted her breasts, cupping them in his hands, and kissed her nipples, eliciting a slight moan from her. Then he slid one hand down between her legs, probed into that bushy patch, and found her wet.

"Oh, God," she said as he slid one fingertip along her moist slit. "My legs . . . are weak . . . please . . ."

Abruptly, he lifted her in his arms, turned, and carried her into the cell block. He chose one of the open cells, entered, and set her down on a cot. He slid one hand down her belly and back into her crotch, rubbing her nipples with the other hand. She reached out, took his cock in her hand, and stroked it.

"So this is what it's like to be in jail," she said.

He chuckled, said, "Not quite," and kissed her.

Miss Jean said to Minnesota, "Who's your friend? Oh, wait, the deputy—"

"Yeah, we're both deputies," Minnesota said, "but don't worry, we're payin' our way."

"Does your friend want to see the girls—"

"I'll pick for both of us," Minnesota said. "Elspeth for him. I'll take Louise."

"Wait in the sitting room," she said. "I'll get them ready for you."

Minnesota and Buck walked into the sitting room. There were a few other men, and half a dozen women walking around wearing next to nothing. Buck's eyes popped.

"You ain't gonna tell me you never been here," Minnesota said.

"N-Not as a customer," Buck said.

"Well, son, you're in for a treat."

"Who's Elspeth?" Buck asked.

"A big, beautiful blonde," Minnesota said, "and I mean big."

"How big?"

"You'll see."

"And what about your girl? Louise?"

"A tall brunette."

"Tall?"

"I like 'em tall," Minnesota said. "Somethin' wrong with that?"

"No, no," Buck said. "Nothin'."

Minnesota leaned over and said, "And I'll tell ya somethin' else."

"What?"

"I like drinkin'," he said, "but nothin' makes me drunk like spending time with a woman—a big, beautiful woman."

"Makes you drunk?"

Minnesota nodded.

"Like I had a bottle of whiskey."

Buck was thinking about that when Miss Jean came into the room.

"The ladies are ready," she said.

"Let's go, son," Minnesota said, slapping Buck on the back.

Lucy lifted her legs and spread them open, giving Clint easy access to her. He moved to the bottom of the cot and leaned on it until his face was right where he wanted it to be. He slid his hands beneath her, gripping her butt, and pressed his tongue to her, tasting her slowly. He licked very slowly up and down her pussy until she was moaning aloud, reaching down to grab the back of his head.

"Oooh," she said as he lapped at her avidly, enjoying the feel of her juices on his face, the tart taste of her on his tongue. "Goddamn. My husband would never do this. And you're so good at it!"

He didn't speak, just continued to use his tongue and lips on her, until he could feel the trembling in her belly and her legs. She went as taut as a bowstring and seemed to stop breathing, then all of a sudden she was thrashing about, crying out, windmilling her legs, and bouncing the cot around, even with their combined weight on it.

He withdrew his face from her hot crotch and said, "And that ain't what it's like to be in jail either."

TWENTY-EIGHT

Clint felt the cot start to give beneath them when he crawled on top of Lucy and entered her. He clasped her to him, got off the cot, and pressed her against the wall. Holding her beneath her buttocks, he took her that way, bouncing her up and down on his cock while she cried out and held him around the neck.

Each time she came down on him, he went into her to the hilt.

"God," she said, "you're going too deep! It almost feels like you're tearing me apart."

"Am I hurting you?" he gasped into her ear.

"Yes," she said, "and don't stop."

He continued to fuck her against the cell wall, pausing only to change sides, turning and walking to the opposite wall and starting again. Then, at one point, he moved away from the wall and just stood in the center of the cell, bouncing her up and down.

"Stop! Stop!" she finally said. "Let me down."

He lifted her off him and set her down on her feet. She immediately went to her knees in front of him, his rigid cock shining with her juices, pulsing with blood in front of her eyes, begging for release.

She took it in her hand and licked it avidly, then opened her mouth and took him in. She moaned and began to suck, sliding her lips up and down him while she pumped her fist on him. The manipulations of both mouth and hand quickly brought him to the brink, but she stopped, releasing his cock but cupping his testicles. She tickled them, stroked them, lick him some more, then took him in her mouth again. This time she did not stop sucking him until he cried out and finished so hard that he stood up on his toes.

When Buck entered the room, he was shocked by what he saw. The blonde on the bed was a mountain of flesh. He stood there staring at her big breasts, pink nipples, the pink slit between her widespread legs.

"Hello, honey," Elspeth said. "Like what you see?"

He wasn't sure. But when he looked at her face and saw how pretty she was, then came closer and saw how smooth her pale skin was, and smelled how good she smelled, he started to see what Minnesota meant.

"Come on, baby," she said. "Get undressed and come to bed with me. I have lots and lots to show you."

Buck quickly got out of his clothes . . .

Louise was not as big a woman as Elspeth, but she was tall, with big breasts, long black hair, and pale skin. And her breasts were topped with the darkest brown nipples Minnesota had ever seen on any whore.

"Not seeing Elspeth today?" she teased him.

"I sent her a friend of mine," he said, undressing. "I was in the mood to share today."

"Gonna share me, honey?" she asked, wiggling her butt.

"Not today, Louise," he said, getting in bed with her. "Today you're all mine."

"You're cute," she said, reaching for him and pulling him to her breasts.

* * *

"Your back looks okay," Clint said as they dressed. "Maybe a little scraped."

"And dirty knees and feet," she said, "but you know what? It was worth it."

"Next time," he said, "a nice soft bed."

"Is there going to be a next time, Mr. Adams?"

"I think there damn well better be a next time, Mrs. Dennison."

"How about some of that coffee before I leave?" she asked, trying to get her hair to look presentable before she went out on the street.

"Sure. I could use some, too." Actually, he could have used a cold beer, and he'd go and get one first chance he got.

He poured two mugs of coffee and handed her one.

"How's it coming?" she asked.

"How's what coming?"

"Your plan to save the town."

"Are you asking as a member of the Town Council?" he asked.

"Just as a concerned citizen."

"It's going fine, then."

"That's all you're going to tell me?"

"There's nothing else to tell," he said. "I'm getting men together to defend the town."

"How many do you have?"

"Now that's something only I'm going to know," he said.

"I suppose that's the smart thing to do," she said, setting the unfinished mug down. "I have to go. When will I see you again?"

"As soon as I can arrange it," he promised.

"I must look a sight," she said, patting her hair and straightening her clothes.

"You look beautiful."

She smiled. "You know the right things to say."

She blew him a kiss, unlocked the door, and left.

TWENTY-NINE

Clint eyed the men assembled before him in his office. Buck Wilby, Minnesota, Commons, Wilkes, and the Prescott brothers. Not much of a force to fight off a gang with, but they'd have to do.

"Everybody well rested, well fed, well . . . whatever it is you did today?"

The Prescott boys nodded.

"Sure," Commons said.

Wilkes just scowled.

Minnesota and Buck both looked as they if they were drunk, but Clint knew that wasn't it. He didn't have time to bother with that, though.

"Can everybody here read and write?"

They all said yes, except Wilkes, who said, "Some."

"I'm going to hand out a schedule I worked on. If you need help reading anything, let me know," Clint said.

He gave them all a sheet of paper with places and times written down. Wilkes actually leaned over to James Prescott, to help him read it. Clint found it odd he didn't seek that kind of help from Commons. He reminded himself to check his wanted posters for any of these men. Not that he would have arrested them, but he would like to know who he was dealing with.

"Any questions?" Clint asked.

"So we're doin' this day and night?" Harley Prescott asked.

"That's right."

"You really think they'll try to ride in at night?" Commons asked.

"No, I don't," Clint said. "I think they're going to want the town to see what's coming, but just in case, I thought we'd set up a night watch."

"How are we supposed to see anything?" Wilkes asked.

"The moon's been bright the last couple of nights, "Clint said. "Should still be for the next few nights. After that . . . we'll see."

They went back to looking at the sheets he had prepared.

"I've also put the schedule up on the wall," he said, "in case anyone loses theirs."

"When do we start?" Buck asked.

"Tonight."

"That puts me on the roof tonight," Buck said.

"I'll believe you at two a.m.," Minnesota said.

Buck nodded.

"Okay," Clint said. "You've got your schedules."

They started to file out. Buck stayed behind for a moment.

"Any more word on Sheriff Harper?" Buck asked.

"No," Clint said, "but the Doc said he's let us know if there was any change, so things must be going okay."

Buck nodded, and followed the others out. Before the door could close, the mayor, Hal Finley, came walking in.

"Sheriff Adams."

Clint still wasn't used to hearing himself called that.

"Mr. Mayor."

"Those your troops?" the Mayor asked. "The men who are going to protect us from the gang?"

"What can I do for you, Mr. Mayor?"

"I'm just checking in," the Mayor said. "You do report to me."

"Technically," Clint said.

"What do you mean?"

"If you had hired me, I'd report to you," Clint said. "But as I told you before, my allegiance is with Sheriff Harper. If I screw up, you can fire him, but you can't fire me."

"I'm—I'm not threatening to fire you," the Mayor said. "I only want to make sure that things are . . . progressing."

"Well, let me assure you, Mr. Mayor," Clint said, "that things are progressing."

"Well . . ." the mayor said, groping for something else to say.

"Anything else I can do for you?"

"Well . . . I just . . . I don't see why you're being so . . . well, rude."

"I'm sorry, Mr. Mayor," Clint said. "I have an intense dislike for politicians. I find most of them . . . crooked, and arrogant." He held his hand up to ward off the mayor's response. "If I've made a mistake and those words don't describe you, I'll apologize when this is all over. But I guess we'll have to see."

"Well, I don't . . . oh, all right," Hal Finley said. "I'll just tell my fellow Council members that things are . . . on track."

"Progressing," Clint said, and then added, "nicely."

"Yes, well . . . thank you."

Clint watched the door close behind the mayor, and wondered if he actually would end up being wrong and having to apologize.

THIRTY

Clint woke the next morning with a feeling. From this point on, they had to be on the alert. The bullet wound one of the Graves brothers had received would have healed well enough by now for him to ride. And they'd certainly had the time to put their gang together.

He got up from his bed and walked to the window. He had spent half his nights in this hotel room, the other half in the office. From this time on, he'd be staying in the office. That meant his guns had to be there with him, too.

He got dressed, took his Colt New Line and his rifle with him as he left the room, and went downstairs for some breakfast.

Since they were staying in the same hotel, it was no surprise to find Wilkes and Commons having breakfast. What still did surprise him was that they were sitting at separate tables.

"'Mornin', Sheriff," Commons said. "Join me?"

Clint looked over at Wilkes.

"Don't worry," Commons said. "He won't think you're playin' favorites. He likes to eat alone."

"And you don't?"

"I don't like to eat with him," Commons said. "But I don't mind eating with others. Please, have a seat."

Clint sat down, ordered steak and eggs when the waiter came over, then poured himself some coffee from the pot on the table. Commons had a plate of ham and eggs and biscuits in front of him.

"And bring hot coffee!" Clint called after the man.

"Yessir."

"Yeah, I like it hot and strong myself," Commons said.

"Do you mind if I ask you what your full name is?" Clint asked.

"I don't mind at all," Commons said, smiling. "That doesn't mean I'm going to answer."

"Fine," Clint said. "Then answer me this. Why are you speaking better today? I mean, more educated."

Commons smiled.

"When I'm around Wilkes, I come down to his level," he said.

"How did the two of you manage to end up . . . partners anyway?"

"We met about five years ago, soon after I came here from the East. Wilkes was born here in the West. We discovered that we work very well together. The only problem was that we didn't get along very well personally."

"Is that why you . . . talk down to his level?" Clint asked.

"It makes things a little easier," Commons said. "We still don't get along, though, so we eat apart, and room apart. We only get together for jobs."

"That's an odd relationship."

"Oh, yeah, it is," Commons said, "but it works."

"What's his full name?"

Commons didn't answer.

"Do you even know it?"

"Actually, no."

"And does he know yours?"

"No."

The waiter came with a steaming plate of steak and eggs, and some more biscuits for Clint. Lastly, he left another pot of coffee.

"Did you check your wanted posters for us?" Commons asked.

Clint nodded around a bite of steak.

"Last night," he said. "Didn't find anything."

"You should have asked me," Commons said. "I would have told you there's no paper on either one of us."

"Do you know there was no paper on him in the years before you met him?"

"I know he hasn't broken the law in the last five years," Commons said. "At least, no big laws."

"I'll have to take your word for it, then."

"Let me ask you something now."

"Go ahead."

"Do you really think the seven of us can hold off the whole gang?"

"Normally, I'd say no," Clint said.

"But this is not a normal situation?"

"I don't think so," Clint said. "We have the facilities of this whole town to back us up, and they're all at our disposal."

"Too bad the men aren't," Commons said. "Has it ever occurred to you to just leave and let them fend for themselves?"

"I'm not doing it for them."

"Ah," Commons said, "the regular sheriff, Harper. You're here out of friendship."

"That's right."

"Admirable," Commons said.

"What's your experience, Commons?"

"With what?"

"That's what I want to know," Clint said. "What do you have experience with? Guns? Are you a carpenter? What skills do you have that we can use?"

"I'll give you one hint," Commons said.

"What's that?"

Commons smiled and said, "Boom!"

"You have experience with explosives?"

Commons nodded.

"Dynamite? Or nitro?"

"More dynamite than nitro, but I've handled it all," Commons said. "Of course, it was years ago."

"Are you still confident you can handle it?" Clint asked.

"Sure," Commons said, "I can handle it."

"Good," Clint said. "After breakfast let's go see what the town has to offer in the way of explosives."

"Suits me," Commons said. "I haven't blown anything up in a long time."

Clint looked at him.

"Hey, it's fun," Commons said. "I miss it."

THIRTY-ONE

Clint and Commons stood to leave, but Wilkes was just starting on a second plate of steak and eggs.

"I'll meet you at the office," Clint said.

"Are you going to have the same conversation with Wilkes?"

"Roughly."

"I'll check around town for explosives," Commons said, "and then meet you at the office."

"Okay."

As Commons started away, Clint grabbed his arm.

"Any advice?"

"Yes," Commons said. "Don't make him mad."

"I'll do my best."

Commons headed for the lobby while Clint walked over to Wilkes's table.

Wilkes looked at Clint, surprised. He'd seen him sitting with Commons, but he just wasn't smart enough to figure out that Clint would come to him next.

"I'm eatin'," Wilkes said.

"I can see that," Clint said. "Mind if I have a cup of coffee with you?"

"What for?"

"Just a talk."

Wilkes looked very put upon, but said, "I guess."

Clint sat, poured himself a cup of coffee. The same waiter came over, but Clint waved him away.

"Didn't you get enough talk from Commons?" Wilkes asked.

"Sure, but that was about him," Clint said. "I want to talk about you."

"Ain't nothin' to talk about."

"Well, there are only seven of us," Clint said. "I need to know what your talents are so I can use them."

"Talents?" Wilkes looked confused.

"What can you do?" Clint asked. "You told me last night you don't use a gun. What do you use?"

Wilkes looked at Clint, then held up his big hands.

"These," he said, then produced a large bowie knife, "and this."

"Commons can handle explosives," Clint said. "Can you do anything like that?"

"Hell, no," Wilkes said, going back to his meal. "I'd blow myself up."

"Anything else?"

"Like what?" Wilkes asked.

"Can you hold your breath a long time, stay up for hours without sleep . . . see in the dark?"

"See in the dark?"

"I'm just digging here, Wilkes," Clint said. "Help me out."

Wilkes took a deep breath, swallowed what he was chewing.

"Look," he said, "when Commons and me are workin' together, I pretty much do what he tells me to do."

"Anything?" Clint asked.

"Anything."

"You do anything he tells you to do."

"That's what I just said."

Clint studied the big man for a few moments, then said, "Well, okay. That's a talent."

"It is?"

"You have no idea," Clint said, standing up. "Finish your breakfast and come over to the office."

"I can do that," Wilkes said, and went back to eating.

THIRTY-TWO

When Clint got to the office, no one was there. With any luck, the Prescott boys were standing watch, according to the schedule. Buck and Minnesota were recovering from their night watch. Commons was finding the explosives he needed. And Wilkes would be along after he finished his second breakfast, unless he was having a third.

He now knew the talents of Wilkes and Commons he could call on. He had an idea about Buck. He still hadn't seen Minnesota shoot, but in every other way the young man seemed competent.

That left Harley and James Prescott. He'd talk to them later in the day, find out if they had any particular talents that he could utilize.

He hadn't given up on finding a few more men, but it seemed unlikely, unless someone rode into town who had been away and didn't know what was going on. He would have felt a lot more confident if he'd had a dozen men instead of seven.

He had sent telegrams out to Bat Masterson and Luke Short, and also to his detective friend in Denver, Talbot Roper. There had been no reply from any of them. The only reason that would happen was if they were each off on their own adventure.

He could have sent telegrams to others, but decided against it. It would take time to track them down, and even more time for them to get to Guardian. No, he was going to have to make due with the men he had, and whatever other men he could pick up along the way.

Buck walked in only moments after he did.

"'Mornin', Sheriff."

"'Mornin', Buck," Clint said. "I thought you'd be asleep."

"I had enough sleep," Buck said. "When the Graves boys hit us, I don't want to miss it because I was asleep."

"I'm glad you're here," Clint said. "I want you and me to walk through town today, see if we can't scare up another volunteer or two."

"Anybody in mind?"

"I still don't know many people in this town," Clint said. "I thought we'd hit some stores, saloons, and just ask."

Buck shrugged and said, "Suits me."

"Have you had breakfast?" Clint asked.

"No."

"Come on," Clint said. "You can grab something on the way."

As Clint and Buck left the office, they almost ran into Wilkes and Commons.

"Where you off to?" Commons asked.

"Going to look for more volunteers," Clint said. "You're going to relieve the Prescotts, right?"

"Soon," Commons said.

"You might as well stay in the office until then," Clint said. "We'll be back as soon as we can, hopefully with more bodies."

"Bodies that can shoot, I hope," Commons said.

"That's the general idea," Clint said. "See you in a while."

Clint and Buck walked down the street as Commons and Wilkes entered the office.

* * *

Once they were in the office, Commons made a pot of coffee. When he turned around, he saw Wilkes sitting at the sheriff's desk, looking through the drawers.

"What are you doing?" he asked.

"I'm just curious," Wilkes said. "I ain't never looked in a lawman's desk before."

"Don't make a mess."

"It's already a mess," Wilkes said. "Hey, here's the wanted posters."

He started to leaf through them.

"Looking for me, or you?" Commons asked.

"Just familiar faces," the big man said. "'Sides, I tol' you there's no paper on me."

"And I told you there's none on me," Commons said.

Wilkes looked at Commons.

"Then there won't be any surprises in here, will there?" he asked.

"No," Commons said, "there won't."

Wilkes continued leafing through the posters. Commons walked over to take a look.

"I know him," he said.

"So do I," Wilkes said. "Nasty. Where was it we saw him last?"

"Sante Fe, I think."

He went to the next one.

"Whoa, I know him, too."

"So do I," Commons said. "I don't think I want to look anymore."

He went back to the stove to wait for the coffee. Wilkes kept going through the posters.

THIRTY-THREE

Clint noticed that Buck was walking with a spring in his step.

"What's going on with you?" he asked.

"Whataya mean?"

"You seem . . . different," Clint said. "What did you do yesterday?"

Buck's face turned red and he said, "Nothin'."

Obviously, it was something embarrassing, but something good. Clint could only think of one thing, and he decided to leave Buck alone about it.

"Let's try over there," Clint said. "The hardware store."

"That's owned by Mr. Murchison," Buck said as they crossed the street. "He's a storekeeper through and through. I don't even know if he can sit a horse."

They mounted the boardwalk and stood in front of the store.

"I guess we'll just go in and find out."

Murchison was not willing to join the acting sheriff's home guard. Clint had decided to use the words "home guard" thinking they'd have an effect on the men in town. He was wrong.

He and Buck talked to several more storekeepers, and

some of their customers, then went into the saloons as they opened for the day, spoke to the bartenders and the owners. It was useless. The men in town were just not willing to risk their lives and go up against the Graves gang. Especially after Clint told them how many men he had so far.

"Wait a minute," Clint said, stopping Buck.

"What?"

They had almost worked their way through the whole town when Clint saw the gunsmith's shop across the street.

"There," he said, pointing.

"I guess that's a possibility," Buck said. "That's run by Ned Dillon. He not only fixes guns, and builds 'em, but he knows how to use 'em."

"Then why didn't you recommend him before?" Clint asked.

"Well . . . he's about sixty."

"So?"

Buck shrugged.

"I thought he was too old."

"I never gave you an age limit, Buck," Clint said. "Come on, let's go talk to him."

As they entered the gunsmith's shop, Clint saw a white-haired man sitting at a workbench. He was bent over an old Navy Colt.

"Be right with ya," the man said. He put down the gun and the brush he'd been using to clean the barrel. "Hey, Buck," he said when he recognized the deputy.

"Mr. Dillon," Buck said. "This here's our new temporary sheriff, Clint Adams."

"Clint Adams?" Dillon said in surprise. "The Gunsmith himself? Well, this is a real honor."

He shook Clint's hand enthusiastically.

"I heard Sheriff Harper got himself hurt, but I didn't hear you were replacing him. Welcome to Guardian. Whataya think of our town?"

"Not much," Clint said.

"Why's that?"

Clint explained to Dillon about the Graves gang, and how nobody in town was willing to step up.

"So you here lookin' for guns?" Dillon asked.

"I'm here looking for men who can use guns, Mr. Dillon," Clint said. "Buck tells me you fit that description."

"I'm not in your league, Mr. Adams, but I can hit what I shoot at with a rifle or a handgun," Dillon said. "What do you need me to do?"

"I need you to be ready, Mr. Dillon," Clint said. "I'm going to need men with guns when the Graves gang comes riding in."

"You need me to do anything else in the meantime," Dillon asked. "Got any more deputy badges?"

"I don't, and that's the truth," Clint said. "I've got some men working for me, standing watch and such, but all I need for you is to shoot when the time comes."

"I'll be ready," Dillon said. "You need to see me shoot. I got a range I set up in the back. Got all kinds of targets."

"You know," Clint said, "I think I'll bring the men in here and use that range, if it's all right with you, Mr. Dillon. I still have to see how they shoot. I can watch you at the same time."

"Hell, bring 'em on in," Dillon said. "And stop calling me Mr. Dillon. The name's Ned."

"And I'm Clint."

The two men shook hands again.

"I'll get the targets ready for you," Dillon promised.

THIRTY-FOUR

When Clint and Buck walked into the office, Commons and Wilkes were lounging around, drinking coffee. In fact, Wilkes had just finished putting things back in the desk. Commons had just made a fresh pot of coffee.

"Coffee's on, Sheriff," he said.

"Thanks, Commons. Buck?"

"Yes, sir, thanks."

Clint walked to the stove, poured two mugs, and handed one to the deputy. He sat in his desk chair, which was warm. Somebody had been sitting there.

"Find anybody?" Commons asked.

"One man. He's the town gunsmith."

"I thought that was you," Wilkes said.

"This man is a real gunsmith," Clint said, not bothering to add that he was also a real gunsmith.

"Can he shoot?" Commons asked.

"We're going find out," Clint said. "He's got a range in the back of his shop, and we're all going over there to try it out. It'll give me an idea of who can shoot, and who can't."

"I already told ya I can't," Wilkes said.

"You said you don't, not you can't."

"Well, the truth is I'm pretty bad."

Clint looked at Commons.

"It's true," the man said. "He's terrible. I wouldn't want to be anywhere around him if you give him a gun."

"That's fine," Clint said. "We're going to try you out with a shotgun."

"When do we do this?" Commons asked.

"In a couple of hours. I want everyone there, so Buck, you and Wilkes go out and find the others. I want everybody at the gunsmith shop in two hours."

"I'll go with Wilkes," Commons said.

Clint was going to object to Commons changing his orders, but the look on the man's face convinced him not to. Commons new Wilkes best.

"Okay," Clint said. "Buck, you go and tell Ned that seven of us will be there in two hours."

"Right, Sheriff."

Buck left, putting his coffee mug down on the desk.

"Come on, Wilkes," Commons said. "Let's go and find the others."

"The Prescotts should be on watch," Clint said. "Minnesota is probably asleep. Wake him up if you have to."

"You got it, boss," Commons said.

Wilkes moved slowly, walking lazily to the door and going out ahead of Commons, who gave Clint a knowing look. Clint decided to allow Commons to handle Wilkes as much as he wanted.

When the office was empty, he went to the gun rack. There were three rifles and a shotgun. He took them down to clean them. He wanted them in proper working order on the range.

The shotgun was a twelve-gauge double-barreled weapon with twenty-inch barrels, the type carried by most stagecoach guards. The rifles were two Winchesters and a Henry.

He settled down to clean them all and check their action, making sure none of them would be disappointing when pressed into service. If one of them was disappointing, it would be because of the man firing it.

When he'd finished with the office guns, he worked on his own weapons, getting them ready for Ned Dillon's range. He didn't shoot targets much anymore. In fact, he rarely fired his weapons anymore unless he was threatened, but this was different. He didn't want to show off for these men, but he wanted them to know what he expected of them.

The last to arrive at Ned Dillon's gunsmith shop was Minnesota.

"Thanks for joining us," Clint said.

"Fell back asleep after those two woke me," the young man said. "Sorry. What's goin' on?"

"Time to show me what you got," Clint said. "Ned here has got a range in the back. You're all going to shoot so I can see what I'm working with."

"What about you?" Minnesota asked. "You gonna shoot, too?"

"We're all going to shoot," Clint said. "Including Ned. He's joining us, which gives us eight men."

"Let's get to it," Wilkes said. "I'll show you how bad I really am."

"Don't sound so proud of it," Clint said.

"I ain't proud," Wilkes said. "I'm just sayin'."

"Let him shoot first if he wants to," Minnesota said. "We can all use a laugh."

"I may shoot lousy," Wilkes said, "but I better not hear anybody laugh."

"Nobody's going to laugh, Wilkes," Clint said. "Come on, let's not keep Ned waiting. He's dying to show us his range."

THIRTY-FIVE

Dillon's range was one hundred feet long. Clay targets were set up against a wooden back wall. Clint introduced Dillon to the men he didn't know. The Prescotts knew him from around town, but he was meeting Commons, Wilkes, and Minnesota for the first time.

"This what we're shootin' at?" Minnesota asked.

"I also have what I call silhouettes," Dillon said.

"Silly-what?" Wilkes asked.

"Watch."

He picked up the end of a rope that was lying nearby and pulled. Immediately, half a dozen wooden cutouts of men's torsos sprang up against the back wall. They weren't really silhouettes because they weren't black, and there was a bull's-eye on each chest.

"Those are good," Clint said. "Leave them up."

"I have replacements when these get all shot up," Dillon said. "They're made of very thin wood."

"Wilkes, you're up first," Clint said.

"I keep tellin' you I'm a lousy shot," the big man said.

"I know," Clint said. "Now show me. Pick up a rifle."

Clint had brought along the rifles and shotgun from the office gun rack.

Wilkes picked up the rifle and toed the line that was drawn on the floor. He levered a round, aimed, and fired, struck the back wall, but didn't hit a target at all. He did the same again, with the same results, then turned toward Clint.

"See?"

"We'll work on it," Clint said. "Who's next?"

"Me," Harley Prescott said. "Okay if I use my own gun?"

"I'd prefer it."

Harley toed the line, drew, and fired off six shots. Dillon walked down to eye the target.

"Four hits, two misses, no bull's-eyes, one killing shot."

"You ever fire your gun at a man before?" Clint asked Harley.

"No."

"Okay," Clint said. "reload and put it away. James? You're up."

James Prescott stepped up to the line, drew his gun, and fired off six shots. Once again Dillon walked down.

"Three hits, three misses, no bull's-eyes, no killing shots."

"Jesus," Commons said, "we're dead."

James gave him a hard look.

"Reload and put it away, James," Clint said. "Commons, why don't you show us how it's done?"

"Gladly."

Commons stepped to the line, drew, and fired.

"Five hits, one miss, no bull's-eyes, three killing shots."

"You've got to do better," Clint said.

"I did better than they did," Commons said.

"They have to do even better," Clint said. "You just have to improve."

"Like this," Minnesota said. He stepped up, drew, and fired six quick shots.

"Six hits," Dillon called out, "five killing shots, two bull's-eyes."

Minnesota stared down at his gun as if it had betrayed him, then holstered it.

"Never holster your gun until you've reloaded," Clint said. "If somebody stormed in here with guns blazing, you'd be dead."

Minnesota didn't like being called out in front of the others, but he drew the gun again, ejected the spent shells, reloaded, and holstered the weapon.

"Why don't you show us how it's done?" Commons suggested.

"Yeah," Minnesota said, "let's see the Gunsmith shoot."

"I quit shooting at targets years ago," Clint said, "but all right."

He stepped up to the line.

"You're all aiming," he said. "You don't have to aim, just point."

He drew his gun, not going for speed, fired six measured shots, then ejected and reloaded even before Dillon could get down to the target.

"Six hits," Dillon said, "all killing shots . . . all bull's-eyes." He turned and looked at Clint. "Perfect shooting."

"Wasn't so fast," Commons muttered.

"It isn't who's the fastest," Clint said. "It's who's the most accurate."

Dillon returned to the line.

"Let's see the gunsmith shoot," Wilkes suggested. "I mean, the real gunsmith."

Dillon looked at Clint, who nodded. He walked over to the side, where a gun belt was lying, picked it up, and put it on. Then he stepped up to the line, drew, and fired six incredibly quick shots by fanning the gun.

Everyone was quiet.

Clint walked down to the target.

"Six hits," he said, "no bull's-eyes, but all killing shots."

He walked back and looked at Dillon, who was reloading. Clint noticed the gun had no trigger in the trigger guard. Dillon had removed it.

"That was incredible," he said.

"No bull's-eyes," Commons said. "What's incredible about that?"

Clint looked at Commons, then the rest.

"He just fanned his gun six times and all six hit the target," Clint said. "It's incredibly hard to hit a target while fanning a gun. It takes skill with both hands, the one doing the fanning, and the one holding the gun."

"How hard could it be just to hit the target?" Commons asked.

"You try it," Clint said.

Commons toed the line, drew, and hired six awkward shots while fanning his gun.

"I can see the results from here," Clint said. "Six misses, all high. When you fan a gun, you jerk the barrel up unless you know how to hold it with your other hand. Like I told you, it takes practice."

"That why you built this range?" James Prescott asked Dillon. "So you could practice?"

"I built it so my customers could try out their guns after I repair them. Or so I can fire a customer's gun and see what's wrong. But since I have it, I come back here and practice quite a bit."

"Okay," Clint said. "Buck, step up to the line."

"I can't match that," Buck said. "Not you or Dillon, or even Commons."

"Just hit what you're shooting at," Clint said.

Buck stepped to the line, drew, and fired six measured shots. Dillon walked to the targets.

"Four hits, two killing shots."

"Reload," Clint said to the deputy. "You'll have to do better."

"What about you, Adams?" Commons asked. "Can you fan a gun and hit what you're aiming at?"

"That's not important," Clint said as Dillon returned.

"Humor us," Commons said. "Let's see how hard it is."

"Okay," Clint said.

"You want my gun?" Dillon asked.

"I'll use my own," Clint said.

Clint stepped up to the line, drew his gun, and fanned six shots at least as quickly as Dillon had. The gunsmith walked to the target.

"Six hits," he said, "All killing."

"Any bull's-eyes?" Commons asked.

"Bull's-eyes aren't important," Clint said, reloading. "Just hit a man where you can put him down."

"Any bull's-eyes?" Commons asked.

Dillon turned to face all the shooters, a look of awe on his face.

"Six."

THIRTY-SIX

The target shattered.

Wilkes smiled.

"I'm gonna have to make more targets," Dillon said.

Clint had made them all shoot for most of the afternoon, in shifts. He'd wanted them to continue to shoot until they were all hitting at least four killing shots out of six.

Now the rest of them were gone, but Wilkes had stayed to continue to shoot with the shotgun. He was enjoying himself.

"Come on," Wilkes said, "set up some more."

"You're shatterin' them every time, Wilkes," Dillon said. "I think you've got it down. Like I said, I have to make more targets."

"Yeah, okay," Wilkes said. "Thanks."

"You better make sure you always have a pocket full of shells. In fact, come with me."

The two men left the range and went back into Dillon's shop. Dillon went behind his counter, rooted around, and came out with a bandolier.

"Wear this across your chest," Dillon said.

He handed the belt to Wilkes, who put it on.

"No shells," the big man said.

"We'll take care of that, too."

He took a box out from behind the counter and began filling the loops in the bandolier.

"There," he said. "How's that feel?"

"Feels real fine," Wilkes said. "Thanks. How much for it?"

"Nothin'," Dillon said.

"Why?" Wilkes asked. "Nothin's for free."

"This is," Dillon said. "After all, we'll probably be shootin' side by side. I don't want you comin' up empty."

"Sure."

"And I also figure right next to you is the safest place for me to be when you start blastin' away."

"Okay," Wilkes said. "Maybe I'll come back tomorrow to shoot some more."

"Sure," Dillon said. "Why not? Practice makes perfect, right?"

"Yeah, thanks," Wilkes said, still not sure what to make of Dillon. "Thanks a lot."

THIRTY-SEVEN

Wilkes walked into the sheriff's office with his new rig on.

"Well," Commons said, "look at you."

Clint looked up from his desk.

"Very good, Wilkes," he said. "Looks good on you."

"I've got to go and relieve Buck," Commons said. "I'll see you both later."

Clint nodded. Wilkes walked to the stove and poured himself a cup of coffee.

"I got a question for you," Wilkes said to Clint after Commons was gone.

"Go ahead."

"Dillon gave this to me."

"So?"

"The belt, and the shells," Wilkes said. "Gave them to me for free."

"And?"

"Why'd he do that?"

"Maybe he thought you needed them."

"Nobody gives away nothin' for free," Wilkes said. "He's up to somethin'."

"He's not up to anything, Wilkes," Clint said.

"But . . . he just gave it to me."

"Sometimes people do that."

"Not anybody I ever knew," Wilkes said.

"Well, don't get used to it," Clint said. "It does happen, but not very often."

"I don't understand it."

"Don't try," Clint said. "How are you doing with the shotgun?"

"Dillon says I'm doin' pretty good."

"As long as you hit something every time you pull the trigger," Clint said, "we'll be fine. Don't you have to relieve Minnesota?"

"Yeah," Wilkes said. He finished the coffee and put the mug down. "Yeah, I do."

"Keep the shotgun with you at all times, Wilkes," Clint said as the big man walked to the door. "Don't ever put it down. I want it to become part of you."

"Fine," Wilkes said, adjusting the bandolier. "I'll even sleep with this thing on."

"That's a good idea," Clint said.

Wilkes shook his, turned, and left.

THIRTY-EIGHT

Frank Graves looked over his gang—his brothers, his cousins, extra members. They were all in the saloon, having been called there by him. There were no other customers in the place.

"Where's Del?" he asked Dudley.

"He's comin'."

Frank looked at the rest. Five brothers, eight cousins, and five other men, including Sammy Holt. Nineteen men altogether. Twenty when Del arrived.

"We're gonna ride tomorrow," he said. "I want everybody well rested, fully outfitted."

"Where are we goin'?" Cousin Arlo asked.

"Guardian."

"Weren't you there already?" Cousin Hasty asked.

"That's where you were shot," one of the other men said.

"We're goin' back," Frank said. "The bank owes us money, and the town owes us even more. We're gonna rob it, and burn it down."

"What about the law?" his brother Clell asked.

"Dudley and me killed him," Frank said.

"They'll have another one by now," his brother Hap said.

"It don't matter," Frank said. "We'll kill him, too. Now get out. Stay sober tonight, and get some rest."

The brothers, cousins, and men began to disperse.

"And stay out of the whorehouse!" he shouted. "I'm talkin' to you, Sammy."

"Yeah, yeah," Sammy said.

When all the men had left, Dudley came over to Frank's table with two beers, and sat down.

"How's the leg?" Dudley asked.

"It's fine."

"Hurts?"

"Yeah," Frank said. "But it's fine. What about our horses?"

"I saw to them," Dudley said. "They're ready to go."

"Del's, too?"

"Yeah."

"Okay," Frank said, "I want you, Clell, and Hap to find Del and bring him here."

"Frank," Dudley said, "Del will be ready. He'll be fine."

"I want to make sure," Frank said. "If we're gonna do this, we need Del."

"If we'd had Del with us the first time, we wouldn't be doin' this now," Dudley said.

"I know," Frank said. "I know."

Minnesota drew and fired at the target, Dillon watching from the side.

"How'd I do?" he asked.

"I can see from here," Dillon said. "Five killing shots."

"And the sixth?"

"Still a hit," Dillon said. "You're where Clint wants you to be."

"I'm not where I wanna be, though," Minnesota said, re-loading.

He holstered the gun and turned to face Dillon.

"I need to fire faster."

"No, you don't."

"Can you teach me to fan a gun?"

"Sure," Ned Dillon said, "if we had months, maybe years."

"Years?"

"It takes a long time."

Minnesota turned to face the targets again.

"What's the problem?" Dillon asked.

"I gotta get better."

"You're good, kid," Dillon said. "I can tell you that."

"But I need to be better!"

"Do what Clint says," Dillon suggested. "Slow down, be more accurate."

"He just doesn't want anybody to be as good as him," Minnesota grumbled.

"Look, son—"

"I ain't your son," Minnesota said. "Go on, old man. Go back to work. I don't need you."

"You'll run out of targets—"

"I'm just about done," Minnesota said.

Dillon shrugged and left him at the range alone.

Minnesota turned to the target, drew quickly, and fired six shots. He walked to the target to check the results. Five killing shots, two bull's-eyes, the sixth shot a hit.

Damn it!

He reloaded, considered putting up more targets, then decided against it.

THIRTY-NINE

Frank looked up when the batwings opened. Dudley, Clell, and Hap came walking in.

"Where is he?"

"He's comin'," Dudley said. "He'll be here."

Frank shook his head. If he was going to have one brother back his play in a fight, it would be Del, but once the fight was over, all he thought about was women, and gambling, and drinking. Del was the middle brother, after Dudley and Frank, older than Clell and Hap.

"All right," Frank said. "Let's eat. Go in the back and tell Diego to bring out some food."

"Okay, Frank," Dudley said. He turned and jerked his head at his brother Hap.

Clell Graves went around behind the bar and drew five beers.

By the time Del Graves showed up, the table was filled with food. He walked in, sat down, and started eating without a word.

"That's it?" Frank said.

"What?" Del asked.

"You're just gonna sit there and eat without sayin' nothin'?"

Del looked at his brother, grinned, and said, "Hi, Frank."

Del looked like a cross between his brothers Dudley and Frank. Not as big as Dudley, built along the lines of Frank, but taller.

"Where've you been all this time?"

"You know," Del said, "poker, girls, more of the same. Don't worry, I'm ready."

"Did the boys fill you in?"

"Yeah, on everythin'," Del said. "Gonna rob the bank, burn the town, kill the lawmen. I got it. You know, if you'd taken me along the first time, none of this would be necessary."

"So I've been told already," Frank said. "Look, the five of us lead this thing. We make all the decisions."

"I thought you made all the decisions, Frank?" Dudley asked.

"For the family," Frank said.

"And the cousins aren't family?" Clell asked.

"They are, sort of," Frank said. "They're cousins, not brothers, like us."

"And the rest?" Hap asked.

"They're just hired hands," Frank said.

"You think they know that?" Dudley asked. "I mean, you think the cousins and the hired hands know their places?"

"They better," Frank said.

"Look," Dudley asked, "once we get this done, this Guardian thing, what's next?"

"I don't know," Frank said. "I ain't looked past Guardian yet."

The other four brothers stopped eating and looked at each other.

"That's not like you, Frank," Clell said.

"Yeah, you usually plan way ahead," Hap said.

"What's goin' on?" Del asked.

"This is all I been thinkin' about," Frank said. "Ever since

I got shot. Just gettin' even with that town. Don't worry, there'll be plenty of jobs after this one."

"Well," Dudley said, "let's just get it done, then. You sure you're ready to ride, Frank?"

"I'm ready," Frank said. "Don't you worry. I'm ready for this."

FORTY

"You want us to do what?" James Prescott asked.

"Camp out," Clint said, "you and Harley."

"Where?"

"North and south of town."

"For what?" Harley asked.

"To keep watch," Clint said.

"What if they come from the east or the west?" Buck asked.

"I don't think they will," Clint said. "I don't think they're going to sneak up on us. The only roads are north and south, and I think they're going to want the town to see them coming."

"So then why do we need to camp out?" James said. "We'll see them from the rooftops."

"I want to see them earlier," Clint said. "I want to know which direction they're coming from so we can get set."

"Set?" Buck asked.

"I've got an idea," Clint said. "Commons has found a store of explosives he can use. We're going to set up some surprises for the Graves gang, but we need to know what direction they're coming from. We need maybe half an hour to get ready."

"So one of us sees them," Harley said, "rides back, and tells you?"

"Right."

"You think we'll see them that soon?" James asked.

"Twelve to twenty men? Riding together? They should scare up quite a dust storm. You'll see them."

"Okay," Harley said, "suppose I camp north and James camps south. And they come from the north. I ride in. How does James know what to do?"

"We'll set up a signal."

"A shot?" Minnesota asked.

"No, the gang might hear a shot," Clint said. "Something else."

"A smoke signal?" Wilkes asked.

They all looked at Wilkes. Everyone had all accepted the fact that he never came up with any ideas.

Until now.

"That's good," Clint said. "They might not see a smoke signal from the other direction."

"So when do we start?" James Prescott asked.

"Today," Clint said. "Saddle up, boys. Take some water and beef jerky, because you'll be making cold camps."

"No coffee?" Harley asked.

"Make a small fire at night if you have to, make some coffee. But during the day the smoke from the fire will be seen."

"Okay," James said.

The Prescotts left the office.

"Won't the smell of coffee be a telltale at night?" Commons asked.

"I think the gang will ride during the day, camp at night," Clint said. "The smell of their own camp will keep them from smelling someone else's. Besides, I don't think is going to take much longer."

"You think they're comin' soon?" Wilkes asked.

"Real soon," Clint said.

"Why?" Commons asked.

"Because this is when I'd do it," Clint said, "as soon as the leg wound heals. You boys just need to stick to your schedules, and split the time the Prescotts would have been on watch."

"And when are we supposed to sleep?" Minnesota asked.

"I told you," Clint said. "This is going to happen soon. Sleep's the least of our worries."

"Then how about you splittin' the watch time with us?" Commons asked.

"Fine," Clint said. "I'll take some of the Prescotts' hours."

"I'm gonna go do some shootin' at the range," Minnesota said.

"Don't forget to relieve me!" Wilkes said.

"I'll be there," Minnesota promised.

The men cleared out of the office, leaving Clint alone. He'd gotten a telegram from Doc Foster earlier in the day. Harper was getting some movement and feeling back in his legs, but he was a long way from being recovered. Clint figured to have all of this cleared up well before Harper got back.

If he was right, the Graves gang was on their way and would get there in a day or two. By the time they arrived, he hoped to have a hot reception set up for them, with the help of Commons.

He and his men had noticed the way the townspeople were avoiding them. When they saw them coming, they stepped aside, not out of fear of them, but out of fear that they might be too close when the shooting started. The others were starting to be bothered by this, especially the Prescotts. They were from the town, and didn't like the way their neighbors and friends were treating them. Maybe Dillon was feeling the same way. He wondered if they'd even stay in Guardian when this was all over.

If there was any town left.

FORTY-ONE

The Graves gang made camp halfway to Guardian.

"Set up a watch," Frank said to Dudley.

"What for? Nobody's after us. It's us who are the ones after—"

"Just do it, Dudley," Frank said. "We don't want any surprises."

"Okay."

"Use the men, not the cousins."

"Okay."

Frank walked to the fire, where Del was drinking coffee. Away from a town, on the trail, Del was a different man. Quiet, moody, but effective.

Frank poured himself some coffee.

"Be there tomorrow," he said.

"Good," Del said. "I want to get this over with and move on."

"You got plans?" Frank asked.

"Shit no," Del said. "You make the plans, Frank. We all know that. I just want you to have a clear mind so you can make us some new ones. We need to make some money, you know."

"I know that, Del."

"This thing in Guardian, this is for your pride. You're mad because they ruined your bank robbery and shot you in the leg. Well, you shot the lawman, didn't you? But you can't let it go."

"Now's not the time for this argument, Del," Frank said. "If you had somethin' to say, you shoulda said it sooner, but you weren't around, were you?"

Del was eating his beans with a spoon, and now he pointed the utensil at his brother.

"I'm backin' your play, Frank," he said. "We all are. But if this backfires, I think we'll have to take a long look at who should be runnin' this outfit."

"Fine," Frank said. "You want to challenge my leadership? Go ahead."

"You guys wanna keep it down?" Dudley asked. "Ya don't want the rest of 'em hearin' you argue."

Frank stretched out his leg and rubbed it. Riding for the first time had made it stiffen up, but he was damned if he'd complain out loud. He picked up his plate of beans and started to eat.

Later, after Frank had turned in, Dudley and Del walked away from the fire and the camp to talk.

"What the hell, Dudley?" Del said.

"I know, Del," Dudley said, "but Frank's the planner. Without him we don't have no jobs, so we gotta go along with him on this. It ain't all personal, ya know. There's still a bank there to be had."

"Well, the take better be worth it, that's all I gotta say."

"You serious about challenging him?" Dudley asked.

"Hell, no," Del said. "I don't wanna lead. Do you?"

"No."

"Clell and Hap, they're too young," Del said. "That's why Frank has the job, 'cause you and me don't want it. And we sure as hell ain't gonna have a cousin runnin' this outfit."

"No chance."

"Okay, then," Del said. "We go along, but he listens to you, so you stay close."

"Don't worry, Del," Dudley said. "I'll be right there with him."

FORTY-TWO

Clint was about to get up from his desk when the door opened and Lucy Dennison came in. It was obvious she was not wearing her sexy underwear this time—or a sexy look on her face.

"I'm kind of disappointed in you, Mr. Adams," she said.

"Why is that, Mrs. Dennison?"

"I thought after my last visit here I'd get some of your attention," she said, "but I haven't heard from you since."

"I've been busy," he said.

"Too busy to be with me?"

"Busy doing my job."

"Come on," she said, "this is not your job. It's Jack Harper's job."

"Right, and since he's not here, it's my job," Clint said. "And we're getting closer to the time the gang will ride in. So you'll have to excuse me if I haven't had the chance to come and play with you."

"Play with me? Is that what you think I want?"

"Yes, Lucy, that's what I think you want me to do—play. And I just don't have the time."

The door opened behind Lucy, pushing her several steps forward.

"Oh, sorry, ma'am," Buck said. "Sheriff?"

"I'm busy, Lucy," Clint said. "I'm sorry."

"So am I," she said archly, and marched out.

"She's mad," Buck said.

"She'll get over it," Clint said. "Or she won't. Right now it doesn't really matter. Did you need me for something?"

"Just wanted to know if you'd like somethin' to eat," Buck said.

"Sure, why not?"

James looked, and looked again. He wasn't sure if he was actually seeing what he thought he was seeing. Whatever decision he made was going to set a lot of things in motion. He knew he had to be right, and he had to be right now if they were going to have time to get things into place.

He looked, and looked still again, and decided this was it. That dust cloud was not natural, and it wasn't man-made.

It was being made by horses.

He mounted his horse and rode hell-bent-for-leather back to town.

FORTY-THREE

James Prescott came riding into town as Clint and Buck were crossing the street.

"They're comin'," he said, dismounting and almost stumbling. "They're comin', Sheriff."

"From the north," Clint said. "All right. Buck, find Commons. James, get to Wilkes and give the signal to your brother."

"Right."

"I'll find Minnesota, and Dillon."

"I think you'll find them both at the range," Buck said.

"Okay," Clint said. "Let's move." He looked at James. "We got half an hour?"

"I hope, Sheriff."

"Okay," Clint said. "After you get to Wilkes, go to the north end of town and stand watch. Tell me as soon as you see something."

"Right, Sheriff."

They all went their separate ways.

Buck found Commons, and they met Clint at the prearranged place.

"They'll be coming in from there," Clint said, pointing up

the main street. "They'll head for the bank first. That gives us an edge."

"So I'll place some charges right in front of the bank," Commons said.

"And in the street," Clint said, "but we won't detonate those until they're trying to ride out."

"Detonate how?"

"With this," Clint said, touching his gun.

"You're gonna detonate dynamite by shooting at it?" Commons asked.

Clint nodded. "From the roof."

"And who's gonna be on the roof to do that?"

"Me and Ned Dillon," Clint said. "Unless you want to try it?"

"No," Commons said. "I saw the two of you shoot at the range."

"The rest of you will take positions on the ground," Clint said.

"Anybody in the bank?" Commons asked.

"Let's put Wilkes in there with his shotgun," Clint said.

"Okay."

"Get the dynamite and plant the charges."

"What if they ride in while I'm still setting charges?"

"You better get started so we make sure that doesn't happen," Clint said.

Commons stared at him.

"Don't worry," Clint said. "I'll be on the roof. I'll have your back."

"You better," Commons said.

They split up.

Frank put his hand up and stopped the gang's progress.

"There it is," he said.

"We see it," Del said. "Let's go and do it."

Frank looked at his brother.

"Let me enjoy this moment," he said. "When we leave

there, we'll have all their money, and the town will be in flames."

"You sure you don't wanna send somebody in first to check it out?"

"No," Frank said, "we don't need to. That town fancies itself a throwback to the days of the old cow towns. That means there's a lot of activity, a lot of trouble, enough to keep a lawman busy. And whoever they have as a lawman ain't gonna be so experienced."

"How do you know that?" Del demanded. "What if they went out and got Wyatt Earp?"

"They ain't had time to get somebody like that," Frank said. "They probably pinned the sheriff's badge on a deputy."

Del looked around, making sure nobody could hear him. He leaned over and lowered his voice.

"You're bein' sloppy, Frank," he said. "You're too anxious. Let me ride in first."

"What for?"

"Just to make sure we're not ridin' into anythin'," Del said. "Any surprises. What's it gonna cost you? Half an hour?"

Frank fidgeted in the saddle.

"Okay," Frank said. "Okay, go ahead. I'll give you twenty minutes."

"It's gonna take me ten to ride down there," Del said.

"Then you better ride fast."

FORTY-FOUR

James came running up to Clint, who was standing on the street while the others got into position. Dillon was already on the roof of the hotel, the highest point in town.

Wilkes was in the bank, looking out the front window. Everyone inside the bank had been sent home.

Harley Prescott, Buck, and Minnesota were in doorways on opposite sides of the street.

Commons was still setting charges.

The townspeople knew something was happening and had left the streets. Clint just hoped the deserted streets wouldn't change the gang's mind as they rode in.

As James came running up, he said, "Single rider comin' in."

"Damn it," Clint said. "I was hoping they wouldn't send a scout in. When he sees the deserted streets, he'll be suspicious."

"What do we do?" James asked.

"Go and take your position," Clint said. "We'll have to hope for the best."

As James left, Buck came running over. Clint told him the problem.

"Can't we get some people on the street?" Buck asked. "Some of us can walk—"

"If he sees a few men on a deserted street, it'll make him even more suspicious," Clint said. "Just go back to your position."

"What are you gonna do?"

"I think I should meet the scout," Clint said.

"Why?"

"I might be able to make him believe I'm alone," Clint said. "If that's the case, the gang will ride in, convinced they're facing one man."

"Will you tell them who you are?"

"No," Clint said, "I'll give him a phony name. One he's never heard of."

"Why don't you tell them you're Wild Bill Hickok," Buck said. "That'll scare 'em."

"I'll give your idea some thought, Buck," Clint said. "Now go ahead, take your position. And remember, nobody fires until I do."

"Got it, Sherriff."

Buck ran back across to his doorway. Clint looked up at the roof across the street, got a wave from Dillon that he was ready.

He walked over in front of the bank, where Commons had finished with his last charge.

"You know," Commons said, "I could've set these so that they'd go off—"

"I know you could have," Clint said. "I know I could have made better use of your talents, Commons, but we've made a play."

"Yeah, okay. What are you doin' down here?"

"They're sending in a scout. I'm going to meet him, try to convince him I'm alone."

"If you can do that," Commons said, "they'll probably roll right in."

"Right."

"Well, good luck."

"Thanks."

Commons left to take his position.

Clint walked to the center of the street to meet the scout. He hoped the others wouldn't panic when they saw him there.

At the end of the street he saw the rider appear, trotting until he spotted Clint, and then slowing to a walk.

FORTY-FIVE

Del Graves saw the single man standing in the center of the street and slowed his horse. As he rode closer, he saw the badge on the man's chest. When he reached the lawman, he stopped.

Clint looked up at the rider, wondering if they'd made a mistake. Maybe he wasn't part of the gang.

"Sheriff."

"What's your name?"

The man settled the question for Clint when he said, "Del Graves."

"I thought so. Where's the rest of your gang?"

"Just outside of town," Del said. "What's your game, Sheriff?"

"No game," Clint said. "I want you and your gang to turn around and ride."

Del looked beyond Clint, then glanced around at the buildings around him.

"Everybody's off the street," he said. "Expectin' trouble?"

"They are," Clint said, "I'm not."

"You must be the new sheriff," Del said.

"That's right. Took over from Sheriff Graves, who you and your men killed."

"And you've been expectin' us to come back?"

"You didn't get the money from the bank the first time," Clint said. "Yes, I've been expecting you to come back."

"And you're ready for us?"

"I am."

Again, Del looked around.

"You alone?"

"Why don't you ride in and see?" Clint said. On the spur of the moment Clint decided that the best way to convince them he was alone was not to answer the question.

"Go tell your brothers and your cousins you met me and don't think they should ride in."

Del smiled.

"You're pretty confident."

"Pick another town, Graves," Clint said. "Don't come in here."

"I'll tell my brothers," Del said, "see what they say. But I think I know."

"Change their minds."

"We'll see."

Del started to turn his horse, then stopped and asked, "What's your name?"

Clint thought, what the hell.

"Wild Bill Hickok."

FORTY-SIX

Del rode back up to Frank and the rest just as it looked like they were getting ready to ride.

"You just made it," Frank told his brother. "What'd you find?"

"A single lawman, standing in the street, waitin' for us," Del said.

"Just one man?"

"It doesn't feel right, Frank."

"You saw just one man?"

"Just one, but there could be more."

"What's his name?" Dudley asked.

"He said Wild Bill Hickok."

"Funny man," Dudley said. "Whataya think, Frank?"

"I think one man is tryin' to stand us off," Frank said, "and it ain't gonna happen."

"He's been expectin' us, Frank," Del said. "I don't like it."

"If he's expectin' us," Frank said, "let's not keep the man waitin'."

Clint was up on his rooftop, across from Dillon, when he heard the sounds of horses approaching. As the gang rode down the main street into town, he counted twenty riders.

*   *   *

The odds were not as bad as he thought they'd be.

The gang rode right up to the bank and started to dismount, looking around. Two riders remained on their horses, handling the reins of the other horses.

Clint couldn't afford to let them go into the bank, not while Wilkes was in there.

As one of the men reached for the doorknob, Clint stood and shouted down, "Hold it right there, Graves!"

Frank Graves dismounted with the others and approached the front door of the bank. This would be the second time he went inside, and this time he intended to leave with the money.

Del and Dudley Graves dismounted and looked around.

"Where is everybody?" Dudley asked.

"They know there's gonna be trouble," Del said. "They're stayin' inside."

As Frank Graves grabbed the doorknob and turned, finding it locked, a voice called out, "Hold it right there, Graves!"

They all looked around them.

"Up here!" Clint shouted.

The men on the ground looked up, spotted him standing there with his rifle.

"That's him," Del said to Frank. "That's the lawman."

"You think one man can stand against us, Sheriff?" Frank asked.

"Probably not," Clint said, "but I'm not one man."

"And I'll bet you're not Wild Bill Hickok either," Del shouted.

"You're right about that," Clint said. "My name is Clint Adams."

Frank looked at Del quickly.

"The Gunsmith?" he said.

"That can't be," Del said.

"Why not?" Dudley asked.

"It just can—"

"It don't matter," Frank said, then looked up at Clint. "It don't matter if you're the goddamned Gunsmith. You can't stand against twenty men."

"As you said, not alone," Clint said, and waved.

Dillon stood up on his rooftop and levered a round to let them know he was there.

The others stood up from their ground positions and did the same so that the sounds of rounds being inserted into chambers filled the air.

Frank looked around.

"Not even ten men," he said, more to himself than to anyone else. "You don't have even ten men!" he shouted.

"Don't try to go into that bank, Graves," Clint said. "Just mount up and ride."

"Clell," Franks said to his younger brother. "The door to the bank is locked. Kick it in."

"Sure, Frank."

Clell Graves walked to the bank door and slammed his foot into it. It sprang open, but as he started to enter, there was the booming sound of a shot. Two loads of twelve-gauge shot slammed him back into the street, his midsection and chest shredded.

"Kill 'em all!" Frank shouted, drawing his gun.

Clint pointed the barrel of his rifle at the first bundle of dynamite buried in the ground and fired. The explosion unhorsed the remaining two bank robbers, and scattered the horses of the others. The concussion knocked several of them off their feet.

Dillon did the same, fired once, and another bundle exploded. There was chaos on the street now, men running, horses screaming wildly and trying to get away.

Clint detonated another bundle, then turned and ran to the hatch on the roof. He wanted to get down to the ground as fast as possible.

Dillon fired and blew up a fourth bundle, but stayed where he was. There were another couple of bundles up the street, in case some of the robbers tried to get away. He stood up and began firing at the bank robbers.

FORTY-SEVEN

On the ground, Buck, Minnesota, Commons, and the Prescott boys began to fire.

Inside the bank, Wilkes was sliding two shells from his bandolier and reloading his shotgun when a man ran into the bank. He was a big man—larger even than Wilkes—with a sloppy gut hanging over his belly, but Wilkes could see the strength in him.

"You killed my brother, you sonofabitch."

Wilkes snapped the shotgun shut, but the man didn't go for his own gun. Instead he charged Wilkes, slammed into him, jarring the shotgun from his grasp. They stumbled back until Wilkes's back struck the wall.

Clint reached the street and drew his gun. Men were running in the streets as the dust from the explosions began to settle. His men were supposed to hold their positions, so that anyone in the street was a bank robber. He could hear the firing of weapons, mostly from his men as the robbers scattered in a panic. He began to fire.

Eventually, the bank robbers began to return fire, but by that time their number had been cut in half. Dillon alone was doing extensive damage from the roof.

Clint rushed to the bank, saw two men standing right in front. He recognized the scout who had ridden in, and the other man strongly resembled him. They both had to be Graves brothers.

In the bank, Wilkes and Dudley struggled against each other. Their chests were pressed together, and they were hand to hand, as if they were wrestling.

Wilkes was thick as a tree trunk and powerful, but Dudley seemed to be at least as strong. Their hot breath mingled, and Wilkes knew he was at a disadvantage because Dudley was still wearing his gun. If the man decided to go for it, he was in trouble.

Dudley Graves was impressed by Wilkes's strength. His anger had caused him to physically engage the man, when what he should have done was draw his gun and shoot him dead.

They were locked in a standoff, so there was only one thing to do.

Abruptly, Dudley released Wilkes's hands and backed away. Wilkes stumbled forward as Dudley drew his gun. But as he stumbled, Wilkes drew his knife. He followed through on his forward motion, and as Dudley came up with the gun, Wilkes buried his knife to the hilt in the man's sloppy stomach. Dudley gagged and pulled the trigger of his gun, discharging it into Wilkes's right foot, and into the floor. Wilkes cried out and backed away, leaving the knife where it was. He fell back on his ass, staring up at Dudley, who had dropped his gun and was grabbing at the knife. He was unable to pull it out before he died.

Several of the robbers grabbed horses and mounted up. They were only concerned with getting away now. As they rode back up the street, Dillon sighted on one of the remaining bundles of dynamite and fired. Commons had buried the last two bundles close together, so as one detonated, it set the other one off. The two explosions killed most of the men and two of their horses. The remaining horses panicked and ran off, trampling several bank robbers as they galloped out of town.

The front of the bank was littered with bodies. Left standing were Clint Adams, and Del and Frank Graves.

Suddenly it was quiet. Clint could hear weapons being reloaded.

"Give it up, boys," he said, "before the shooting starts again."

The two men glared at him. Frank was angry, at Clint, and at himself for taking all this so personally. His anger had brought them all to this.

Del was just angry with his brother, for much the same reason.

"You suckered me," Del said.

"You suckered yourself," Clint said. "Which of you shot Sheriff Harper?"

"I did," Frank said. "I put two in his back. I killed him."

"You didn't."

"What?"

"He needed surgery, but he's okay. He's still sheriff of this town. I'm just wearing the badge until he comes back."

"You're a liar."

"No, I'm not," Clint said, "And you'll see, because you'll be in jail when he comes back. He'll want to come and see you."

"I'm not going to jail."

"Frank—" Del said.

Both Graves brothers were holding their guns in their hands, down at their side, as was Clint.

"Don't do it, boys," Clint said. "In all the excitement you might have forgotten to reload."

Del looked down at his gun, frowning. Had he reloaded?

But Frank didn't look down. Frank was determined not to go to prison.

"Fuck you," he said, and started to bring the gun up.

Clint shot him in the chest before he got halfway. Frank fell to the ground, dead. Del looked down at him, then at Clint.

"Which one are you?" Clint asked.

"Del."

"You're the last one, Del," Clint said. "Want to try it?"

The rest of them—Commons, the Prescotts, Minnesota, and Buck—had come out from their positions and were now standing behind Clint. Dillon was still on the roof, his rifle trained on Del.

"What do you say, Del?"

At that point Wilkes limped to the open door of the bank, shotgun in hand, and leaned against it. Del didn't see him, but he could feel him.

He dropped his gun.

"Good decision."

Looking around at his dead cousins and brothers, Del wasn't so sure.

FORTY-EIGHT

Clint came out of the hotel several days later with his sad-dlebags and rifle. Eclipse was standing quietly in the street. Clint tossed his saddlebags over the big Darley Arabian's back and slid his rifle into the scabbard.

Buck came walking over with Minnesota. They were both still wearing their deputy's badges.

"Sure you won't change your mind?" Buck asked.

"Why don't you change your mind and put that sheriff's badge on," Clint said. "You earned it."

"Naw," Buck said, "I ain't ready to be sheriff. I'll just keep wearin' this badge until Sheriff Harper gets back. Does he know you're leavin'?"

"I sent him a telegram, got one back from Doc Foster," Clint said. "Jack understands. It's time for me to move on."

He looked at Minnesota.

"What about you?" he asked. "You going to keep the badge on?"

"For a while," Minnesota said. "Think I'm gonna stick around, spend some more time at Mr. Dillon's range."

"Can't hurt," Clint said. "What about the Prescotts?"

"They're back to odd jobs," Buck said.

"Commons and Wilkes?"

"Left early this mornin'. Gonna move on to a town with a doctor, get Wilkes's foot looked at. Still had the bandage you put on it."

"Were they arguing?"

"Oh, yeah," Buck said.

Clint nodded. That was a partnership he didn't understand, but he was hoping each man might have learned something over the last couple of weeks or so.

Clint mounted up.

"Oh, Clint," Buck said. "That telegram say how the sheriff is doin'?"

"He's on his feet," Clint said. "Not ready yet for a long train and stage journey, but soon."

Buck stepped forward, extended his hand.

"Thanks for everything," he said.

"Sure thing, Buck."

"Sheriff," Minnesota said, shaking his hand.

"Not anymore," Clint said. "Just Clint Adams again—the way I like it."

Watch for

SOMEONE ELSE'S TROUBLE

345th novel in the exciting GUNSMITH series
from Jove

Coming in September!

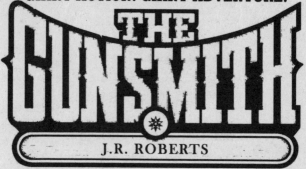

GIANT ACTION! GIANT ADVENTURE!

THE GUNSMITH

J.R. ROBERTS

Little Sureshot And
The Wild West Show
(Gunsmith Giant #9)

Dead Weight
(Gunsmith Giant #10)

Red Mountain
(Gunsmith Giant #11)

The Knights of Misery
(Gunsmith Giant #12)

The Marshal from Paris
(Gunsmith Giant #13)

Lincoln's Revenge
(Gunsmith Giant #14)

penguin.com/actionwesterns